PUFFI

Editor:

MIKE

Remember Jim Woolcott, the boy who had the terrifying adventures with his friend Soldier in *Run for Your Life?* (It's been on television, and it's in Puffins too). Well, here he is again in another thrilling adventure, this time shared with his cousin Mike.

It all began when the art master at their school, a dotty character named Moggy, began looking around for old books and documents to put in an exhibition about the history of the town and the school and, by discovering one particular old document, trod right on the toes of a bunch of greedy speculators who wanted to pull down the old parts of the town and make themselves a fortune putting up huge great skyscrapers instead.

The speculators were not only greedy, they were ruthless too. Stealing the precious document from the library meant nothing to them, nor did bashing the aforesaid dotty art master on the head and landing him in hospital, and that certainly wasn't all they would do to the boys if they could catch them.

Breathtaking, nightmarish, this wonderfully told story, ending in a supremely exciting race against time, is a must for any boy who likes books with action and plenty of it.

For readers of ten and over.

DAVID LINE

Mike and Me

PUFFIN BOOKS

Puffin Books Penguin Books Ltd, Harmondsworth, Middlesex, England
Penguin Books, 625 Madison Avenue, New York, New York 10022, U.S.A.
Penguin Books Australia Ltd, Ringwood, Victoria, Australia
Penguin Books Canada Ltd, 41 Steelcase Road West, Markham, Ontario, Canada
Penguin Books (N.Z.) Ltd, 182–190 Wairau Road, Auckland 10, New Zealand

—

First published by Jonathan Cape 1974
Published in Puffin Books 1976

—

—

Made and printed in Great Britain
by Hazell Watson & Viney Ltd,
Aylesbury, Bucks
Set in Linotype Juliana

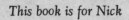
This book is for Nick

I

The first I heard about Mike's instinct we were up in the art room working on the mural. We'd been working on it five weeks and Moggy said we could start colouring-in then. He's the art master, Moggy. There were thirty of us working on the mural, and it was in six panels. Moggy came up to where Mike and I were working and watched for a bit.

'What's up?' he said.

Mike was shaking his head and coming out with these little groans, just under his breath. He can do it for hours.

'I can't keep to the lines,' he said.

'That's all right,' Moggy said. 'Forget the lines.'

'I'll ruin it for the others.'

'No, you won't. You're doing fine. You're an intuitive worker, Mitchell.'

'I am?' Mike said.

'Oh, yes,' Moggy said, and drifted off, nodding his head.

Mike watched him with his mouth open, then he said, 'What's intuitive?'

'He means you're a nit,' I said.

'No, honest.'

'Honest.' He'd gone over my red with his green. 'A big nit. In-tuitive. Unteachable.'

'I don't believe it.'

'All right, ask him.'

'All right, I will.'

Moggy wandered by five minutes later and Mike said, 'Sir?'

Moggy looked at him a bit old-fashioned. He doesn't like

7

being called sir. He's an artist, Moggy. He's R. S. Morgan. 'What is it?' he said.

'What's intuitive?' Mike said.

'Intuitive? It's – intuitive,' Moggy said. 'You have a strong instinct.'

'Is that right?' Mike said, worried.

'You mean you didn't know about it?'

'Not till you just mentioned it,' Mike said. 'No. Not at all.' He was looking more worried than ever.

'Well, it's a way of looking into things. It's instinct. It's a natural gift.'

Mike didn't say anything but his face went bent. Nobody'd ever told him he had a gift before.

'What you want to do with a thing like that,' Moggy said, 'is let it rip. You don't want to confine it, Mitchell. You want to give it scope.'

'Don't confine it. Let it rip. Give it scope. Yes, sir,' Mike said. 'That is, thanks. I mean, blimey!'

He's six foot one, Mike. He's fifteen. A lot of people think he's a dope because he's fifteen and still in our class. He isn't a dope. He was ill in hospital for a year and it held him back. He still limps a bit but you don't notice much. He does, of course. He notices everything like that, people thinking he's a dope and laughing at him and calling him Nellie because he won't get in a fight. He could flatten anyone if he got in a fight, but he won't. He's my cousin.

He came round with his Mum that night. They're sisters, his mum and mine, and they always have a lot to yatter about. We waited till they started and went up to my room. My mother saw us go but she only gave me a look.

'What's the trouble?' I said to Mike. He was looking depressed again.

'Nothing.'

8

'The Cobbler?'

'A bit.'

'Well, blow *him*!'

'Yeah.'

The Cobbler was the Head, a swine called Cobbridge. The snag was, Mike wasn't brilliant. He'd already been told by the Cobbler he might have to go after the July exams. Still, it wasn't July yet. It wasn't even Easter yet.

'How about that instinct, then?' I said, to cheer him up.

'How about that?' Mike said.

'He's a nut-case, Moggy.'

'He's a decent geezer. He's got a one-man show coming off, you know.'

'Who told you?'

'He did. He asked me to stay and look at one of his pictures for him. Because of my instinct,' he said proudly. 'He wasn't too sure of something in it.'

'What was it?'

'I wasn't too sure, either,' Mike said. 'I think it was an anchor. You know Moggy's pictures.'

Everybody knew Moggy's pictures. They were crazy. He used to stick things on them, old cans and bicycle pedals and bits out of the newspaper. They were part of the picture. He's a decent nut-case, though, Moggy, so you always say you like them.

'He's stuck an *anchor* on a picture now?'

'Yeah. It's a bit way-out. He's got another thirty pictures just like it. It's his first one-man show.'

'He better make the most of it. He'll never have another.'

It seemed to have got his mind off the Cobbler, though, so I let him rattle on a bit, and then said. 'O.K., work.'

'Work,' Mike said, looking ill again.

'French.'

'French,' Mike said.

He got his book out and I had a look in it to see what Fleming had to say this time, '70% *A great improvement. Keep this up!*' Fleming had written.

'Well, things are looking up,' I said.

'Yeah,' Mike said.

I opened my book.

I'd got 70 per cent, too.

My mother ironed a shirt for me after they'd gone, and she seemed to be taking her time over it. She opened her mouth once or twice without saying anything, so I lapped up my cocoa fast and said, 'O.K., good night.' I knew what she wanted to say.

'Just a minute,' she said.

'I'll wash the cup.'

'Never mind the cup. And come back here. I want to talk to you.'

I groaned under my breath.

'It's about Mike,' she said.

I groaned again.

'And stop that. You know what I'm talking about. It's no good giving Mike the answers.'

'Yeah, O.K.'

'It isn't O.K. And don't *say* O.K. Don't say yeah, either. If you mean yes, say yes. What's the use of him knowing answers to problems he can't understand?'

'No use,' I said.

'Don't be clever with me!' she said, getting in a temper.

'I was just agreeing with you!'

'I know all about that! You're so clever you'll be kicked out of that school with him. After all the sacrifices I've made and *am* making to keep you there.'

'Oh, Gawd!' I said, but not aloud.

'If your father was alive he'd know how to deal with you.

Can't you see that someone will notice Mike's exam results aren't the same as his homework results?'

'Yeah. Yes,' I said, and suddenly got fed up. 'Look, what's wrong with giving old Mike a shove?'

'Nothing, if you shove him the right way. He's a nice boy, Mike, but he's not academic. He'd be happier at another school.'

'Is that the Cobbler's sacred view?'

'Who?'

'Our brilliant Head, the Blessed Cobbridge.'

'Yes, it is. And don't talk to me like that.'

'What does Aunt Freda think?'

'She's beginning to think the same. As a matter of fact,' she said, not looking at me and beginning to iron a bit harder, 'she doesn't *want* you to help him any more. She knows you're not supposed to, and that it's a risk for you.'

She said the last bit fast, so I knew she was the one who raised the question of risk. Poor old Mike. Everyone was on his back now. It looked as if an extra shove was going to be needed, and this was such a drag I took the shirt without a word and went up to bed, brooding.

2

In things like art or woodwork, when you can work next to anyone, Mike worked next to me. I didn't mind. It caused problems with others, like my friend Nixon, but I couldn't help it. He's had bad luck, Mike. They went to live in Scotland but his old man got killed in an accident so they came back. He'd been in a good school in Scotland, so they got him in ours, but he'd hardly joined when he fell ill and had to go to hospital for a year. All this made him nervy so he stuck close to me. I couldn't shove him away.

A funny thing was, he grew like mad in hospital. He grew inches there, and before they let him out he had to do physiotherapy, a lot of exercises. He did leg exercises and arm exercises and chest exercises, and it's a pity they didn't dream up a few for his brain as well. Still. He's fantastically strong. In woodwork once, we had to shift benches and it took four kids to each bench. Mike did his by himself.

It was in woodwork the next thing happened. He said, 'Jim, can you help me tonight?'

I'd been helping him every night so I just looked at him.

'It's a job down the Lanes,' he said.

He said it in a whisper but I looked round to see who was listening. You're not supposed to go down the Lanes. One kid got six weeks' detention for being there.

I said, 'Are you crazy?'

'There's been a fire at the place Moggy's having his exhibition. He can't open till it's cleaned up.'

'Let him clean it.'

'No, honest. He'll miss his chance. We got to help.'

'*He* said he wants us to help?'

'He wouldn't turn us away. I'll call for you after tea and we'll go.'

'*We* won't!'

'Woolcott!' It was Pike. He's the woodwork master, Pike. He picks on me. He's a twit. 'If you talked less and worked more, you'd get on better. What's this supposed to be?'

'It's a tie-rack, sir.'

He knew it was a tie-rack. I'd been making the flaming tie-rack for over a year. He hadn't let me take it home when the others took theirs: I'd sawn it wrong or planed it wrong or done something else wrong. It made me sick to look at it every week.

'Is that what it is? Is that what it is?' he said. He always repeats himself. He's an evil old swine. He blinks when he's excited. 'All you're doing, you're ruining wood. Know what wood this is? Know what it is, eh?'

'Mahogany, sir.'

'Yes. Mahogany. And planed against the grain, you little fool. What you think you're doing with it? What you doing with it, eh?'

'I'm making a tie-rack out of it,' I said.

Pike started to blink. 'Sir,' he said. 'Call me sir. Don't forget it. Don't forget it, eh?'

'All right,' I said. 'Sir.'

Just then someone said, 'Haw-haw-haw,' and Pike swung round.

'Who said that?' he said.

Nixon had said it. He'd been waggling his ears, too. Pike turned so fast he was still doing it. Nixon pretended he was scratching his ear.

'Nixon,' Pike said. 'It's you, Nixon.'

'Me, sir?' Nixon said. He looked down at himself. 'Why, yes, sir,' he said, a bit wonderingly. 'Of course it's me. Who else could it be, sir?'

Pike started blinking like mad. He's a bit scared of Nixon.

Nixon's old man is one of the school governors. He's our doctor, Dr Nixon.

He said, 'Don't be cheeky, Nixon. That was you making that noise. I know it was.'

'Noise, sir?' Nixon said. 'I didn't hear any noise. Did you hear a noise?' he said to the kid next to him. The kid said he didn't, and in no time everyone was asking if they'd heard a noise. Nixon started taking a scientific interest in it. He asked Pike if it might have been the drains, or a bench creaking, or even Pike's digestion. Pike nearly went up the wall.

'What *kind* of noise was it, sir?' Nixon said, getting more interested every second.

He was trying to get Pike to make the noise himself, but Pike wasn't having any. The upshot was that Nixon got sent out, and I got sent out with him for laughing. He always creases me up, Nixon, and he knows it. I had an idea he was trying a bit harder this time for my benefit because we'd had a row lately, and he wanted to make it up. He's a complicated character, Nixon.

Outside, I was still creased up, and he said, 'Honest to God, it's a wonder he's not in a padded cell.'

'A lunatic,' I said.

'A genuine half-wit.'

'He counts on his thumbs.'

'On his *toes* . . . Here,' Nixon said, 'I'm definitely getting that bike.'

'Honest?'

'No kidding. Guaranteed. Dad promised.'

'Well, great,' I said. There'd been a lot of talk about this new bike. I was supposed to be getting the old one. He was going to take four quid for it. My mother wasn't too crazy about it. She said it sounded as if he was giving it away; which wasn't very likely. He has a lot of dough, Nixon, but he's careful with it; only he'd told me a week ago the chap in the bike shop had offered him five quid for it, and I'd stayed awake wondering if it was true, and if so why he'd told me. He's like that, Nixon. He keeps you guessing. Still, a bike's a bike, so I waited for him to say something else. He said 'How about coming round tonight – get your hand in on the old one?'

I said, 'O.K.,' still watching him. He rarely lets you ride his bike. He rarely lets you use any of his things. It looked as if he meant it, and my head swam.

He said, 'After tea, then?'

I said, 'Yeah. Fine,' and suddenly remembered Mike and said, 'I've got to check something first. I'll tell you after school.'

'Check what?'

'I was doing something with Mike. I'll try and put him off.'

I knew right away it was a mistake to say I'd only try. Nixon didn't stop smiling but he said, 'Skip it, then.'

'No, it'll be O.K.'

'No – carry on.'

'It's only old Mike.'

'Anyway, I just remembered,' Nixon said. 'I'm doing something tonight.'

'Look, I can guarantee it.'

'Some other time.'

'Tomorrow?'

'I'm busy tomorrow.'

'Sunday?'

'And Sunday.'

I didn't say anything, and he didn't, either. We just stood not looking at each other till Pike sent out to say we could come in again.

I had a look for him after school, all the same, but he wasn't there. Soldier was there. He was hanging about waiting for me. He's a foreign kid, Soldier. His name is Szolda, really. I helped him in a bit of trouble once and he's hung around ever since. He said, 'Hi, Woolcott.'

'Hi.'

'I've got some foreign stamps for you at home.'

'Thanks.'

'Want to pick them up on the way back?'

'I can't now.'

'Oh,' Soldier said, and looked hurt. He doesn't smile to hide his feelings like Nixon. He just looks hurt. Suddenly I got in a temper with him, and with Nixon, with both of them, for having to watch what I said, so I shouldn't hurt their feelings. Nobody bothered too much about mine.

He said, 'I haven't seen you much lately.'

'I been busy lately.'

'You want me to bring the stamps round to your place?'

'Yeah, all right,' I said, and as soon as I said it knew I could have put it better, so I grunted and said, 'Thanks. You don't have to bother, though.'

'No bother,' he said, and grinned.

With him it's like giving a dog a bone.

My mother wasn't in when I got back. She doesn't come in till after six. She has an afternoon job at a dress shop. She leaves stuff for me to eat. I didn't feel like anything so I just had a glass of orange and went out the back and climbed the elm tree and lay out in it, brooding.

I'd left the back door open so I could hear if anyone rang the doorbell, and after a while it rang. I leaned down and looked along the passage. There was a long streak standing the other side of the front door panel that could only be Mike. I let him wait a while and then got down and let him in.

He'd taken his cap off and changed his jacket, so there were no school badges. You wouldn't have taken him for a school kid at all, he's too tall. He'd scrubbed his face and was looking very busy and important.

He said, 'O.K., ready?'

I hadn't made my mind up, but I made it up then. I said, 'Yeah, O.K., why not?'

3

We took the bus to George Square and cut down the back streets to the Lanes. It's heavy round there. There are rows of pin-table saloons and betting shops. There'd been schemes to clear it up but nobody'd been able to agree how to do it. The thing is, part of it is Auldhouses, and they're very old. They're historic. They were put up as almshouses for old women in Elizabethan times. They aren't almshouses now and there are no old women around, but it's Trust land and you can't do what you want with it. It's complicated to explain, so I'll have to do it later. Anyway, we got down there.

It's a maze of streets, behind the market area, and we looked around and found the gallery. It wasn't a proper gallery. It's Lepic's, the picture-framer's, in Auldhouses. He has exhibitions at the back of the shop. It was a mess now. The windows were broken and the floor inside covered with rubbish. There must have been half a ton of rubbish, and the fire hoses had left pools of water in it, so this terrible smell was hanging everywhere.

We held our noses and tramped through the rubbish, and saw Moggy inside. He was standing in his duffel-coat with his hands in the pockets. He was just standing there looking around and swearing to himself. We let him do it for a bit and then Mike cleared his throat and said, 'Mr Morgan.'

Moggy carried on swearing.

'Good evening, Mr Morgan,' Mike said. 'We've come to help.'

There was no light in the shop and Moggy couldn't see us properly. He just stared for a moment and said, 'Who is it?'

'Woolcott and Mitchell.'

18

'Woolcott and Mitchell?' Moggy said. He seemed in a bit of a trance and the way he said it, it sounded like Laurel and Hardy.

He carried on staring, and nobody said anything till the back door opened and Lepic came in from the yard. He came skipping in and he seemed to break into a dance. It took a moment or two to see he was just in a fantastic rage. He started leaping up and down in the rubbish like a monkey. He was swearing worse than Moggy and he was howling at the same time.

'Oh, they can do what they want with Lepic,' he howled. 'They can do anything with him!'

He's a weird little geezer, Lepic. He wears a beret and always has a bit of fag stuck in his mouth. You see his photo in the paper sometimes. He's written a book about Auldhouses, and it's in the library. From what he was screaming, between the howling, he'd just rung up the insurance company from next door, and it had nearly sent him round the bend.

'It's only old Lepic!' he howled. 'I'm too small, I only paid insurance here fifteen years without a claim, so who has to worry about me?'

'Hang on, Mr Lepic,' Moggy said. 'Take it easy. Did you ask them about the salvage people? Did they say when they can send round and clear up?'

'It won't be this week!' Lepic howled. 'And they can't even give me a date for next. It's because I'm not selling soap-powder, you see, or groceries. It's only art I'm selling, that's all . . . Oh, look at my poor walls!'

He'd had hessian sacking on the walls as a background for the pictures. It was all burned off now and bits of the wall had crumpled off with it. Lepic stumbled over the rubbish and started stroking the wall and crooning to it as if it was a baby.

Mike cleared his throat again.

'Have you got a box?' he said to Lepic.

'Go away,' Lepic said.

'A big one. Like a tea-chest. Have you got anything like that?' Mike said.

'Yes, I have. Out the back. And keep your thieving hands off it!' Lepic said sharply. 'Who are you, anyway? What do you want?'

'We're from Mr Morgan's school,' Mike said. 'We've come to clear up for his exhibition.'

Moggy had snapped out of his trance but I don't think he cottoned on till just then who we were.

He said in astonishment, 'Mitchell, is it you, Mitchell?'

'Yes, Mr Morgan. And Woolcott.'

'Well, go away, both of you. Go away at once,' Moggy said. 'You're not supposed to be here.'

He was quite right and I passed him a silent vote of thanks. Lepic's howling had attracted a few people to the open doorway and they were grinning in. They'd very likely attract a few more, and I remembered the kid who copped the six weeks' detention; also what my mother was likely to say.

It didn't seem to bother Mike. He said, 'It'll only take an hour or two to get this off the floor, and then we can see what to do about it.'

'No, we can't,' Moggy said sombrely. 'It was a nice thought, Mitchell, but it isn't like that. This is for other people. We can't touch it till they find out how it got this way.'

'How it got this way? There's been a fire, hasn't there?' Mike said. It was too dark to see his face but I could imagine the puzzled frown there. He's a bit thick up top sometimes, Mike. I'd figured right away what Moggy was talking about. It wasn't the only fire there'd been round there. I was trying to think what else I'd read about the fires when I became aware of a couple of other things.

One was that the fellows in the doorway had started laughing out loud at what Mike said, and the other that little Lepic had started yelling again. He seemed to be yelling at them. He yelled, 'Yes, they can start twenty fires! They can start fifty! They still won't get me out of the place. Not unless I go up with it!'

The laughing got louder round the doorway, and one of the geezers, I couldn't see which, called out, 'Is that an offer, darling?' and the hairs on the back of my neck stood up. I suddenly remembered what a hairy place this was at night. There'd been a lot of stories about it lately. Even the police only came down in cars or in pairs. It seemed a great place to get away from fast, and I grabbed Mike's arm and gave it a yank; only he got the wrong idea again and said loudly, 'Yeah, what's so funny?' and he walked right up to the doorway and told them so.

'Mitchell!' Moggy said. 'Come here, Mitchell.'

'Yes, Mitchell – trot along, Mitchell,' one of the yobs said, and another said, 'Get lost, Mitchell,' and another said, 'Have a banana, Mitchell,' but Mike went, all the same, and Moggy said quietly, 'Mitchell – and Woolcott, are you listening? I want you to get out of here right away. I want you to go out the back way.'

'Why should we go out the back way?' Mike said.

'Because I'm telling you to,' Moggy said. 'Do it quietly. Don't run. Just walk normally, as if you're going to see something. But do it immediately. Mr Lepic and I will have a word in the doorway while you're doing it.'

Mike started to say something, but I gave him a swift knee in the behind, and he got moving. He went through the back door and I went after him, into a little dark yard.

'Hello,' Mike said. 'Here's the tea-chest. And a bucket, as well. We could have cleared it easy. Wait a minute, there's two buckets!'

I didn't care if there were fifty buckets, but the big idiot started bashing about with them to see if there wasn't a third tucked away in one.

I said, 'Mike, get moving fast. Don't make a row. They'll hear us at the front!'

'What if they do? The fire's got to be cleared up some time, hasn't it? They'll come in very useful, these buckets.'

I thought I'd go out of my mind if he kept finding buckets. I said, 'Look, those guys at the front probably *started* the fire. We've got to get away from here. Moggy said so!' I said the last as some kind of appeal, because he was still admiring buckets. He didn't put the buckets down but he turned to me in amazement.

'They started the fire?' he said. 'Why should they? What are you talking about? I know ... it's one of your jokes, isn't it?'

I could have strangled him, but I said, 'Yeah, Mike, that's it. And we'll have a good laugh about it later. Only I just got to go somewhere now, so if you've decided to live here, could you get out of the way so I can open the back door?'

'I can open the back door,' Mike said, and he did, and knocked over the dustbin that was standing there. He'd made enough clatter before but it was nothing to the row this kicked up, and I stood there feeling myself freeze and wondering whether it was better to hide in the yard somewhere. They were bound to have heard the row, and what with Moggy and Lepic having their chat in the doorway, it didn't take a genius to work out that we were probably trying to get out the back. They might come and have a look just for a bit of sport.

Mike was putting the dustbin right and tut-tutting at the carelessness of people who left dustbins in doorways, and he rubbed his hands and said, 'O.K., come on if you're coming,' and set off up the alley, and I followed him, and hadn't gone more than twenty paces before I saw I was dead right. They were waiting at the end of the alley. There were four of them, about twenty years old, maybe older, and they were grinning.

I said softly, 'Mike,' and tugged at his wind-cheater. He turned, and I said. 'Mike, don't say anything to them. Don't annoy them or anything.'

He said, 'Why should I annoy them?' And I said, 'O.K., well don't, anyway. Just keep walking, and if they get in the way walk round them. Don't push.'

He said, a bit indignantly, 'I wouldn't want to push anyone. They're just ordinary chaps – they don't mean any harm. Although what's so funny about a fire?' And I said, 'Yeah, well forget that, too. Particularly forget that. Just keep on steadily,' and he did.

They didn't bunch up to stop us getting out. They just stood and watched with grins on their faces as if we were a comic turn, and one of them said. 'Well, we keep on meeting, Mitchell, don't we? Fancy you being here.'

Mike didn't say anything, and another one said in a deep voice, 'Evenin' all!' Mike still didn't say anything, but I felt a fool walking on poker-faced, so I muttered, 'Evening,' and they let us through and we turned into the street.

Mike kept on pretty steadily, and they kept on steadily with us, two on each side, and one of them started calling, 'Hup two three four! Hup two three four!' as if we were marching, which had them laughing more than ever, and I felt such a flaming idiot, as if we were girls on a Sunday-school outing and rude kids were ribbing us, that I started whistling.

'They're musical!' one of them said.

'They're off to a music date.'

'And they're late. In a hurry, aren't they?'

'Must be a fire somewhere.'

The last crack really creased them up, and I saw Mike biting his lip, but it wasn't because of the crack. The chap on his side had noticed the limp and was limping himself now, only in an exaggerated way as if one leg was about a foot shorter than the other, and as soon as the others saw it they started doing it, too.

I didn't say anything, and just prayed he wouldn't either. The alley had only brought us out into Auldhouses. There were two rows of the little buildings, facing each other, and we still had to cut through another lane before there'd be more people around. I remembered people had been found beaten up in the gutter round here, and my breath was coming a bit funny as we crossed over and turned into the lane. Mike seemed to have gone a bit stiff, too, and I saw he was trying not to limp; and that the others had noticed it and were doing it even more.

'Streets a bit bumpy round here, Charlie, aren't they?' one of them said, and the one called Charlie said, 'Yeah, you find yourself going up and down. Even Mitchell's doing it too, look,' and then Mike seemed to go mad.

He just stood in the lane and sort of shook himself. He yelled, 'You stupid idiots! What's so funny in the way a person walks?' Only the thing was, his voice had started breaking a few weeks ago, and when he was upset it came out as a yodel, and I thought the four characters were going to fall apart. They started pointing to him and falling against each other, laughing, and one of them sang out, 'Oh, Miss Mitchell! We've gone and offended her!' And another wheezed, 'We never meant it, darling!'

But Mike hadn't finished yet. He was panting and it was hard for him to yell, but he managed to get out, 'And I don't see anything funny about fires, either!'

'No! Horrible, nasty things!'

'Or in starting fires!' Mike said.

'Who'd do a thing like that?'

'I hope you're still laughing in prison,' Mike said. His voice was still yodelling up and down so much it sounded as if he was sobbing, but that wasn't why they stopped laughing.

I said, 'O.K., Mike, come on.'

'No, wait a minute,' the one called Charlie said.

I said, 'He didn't mean it. We're going home now.'

'No, I want to look at him,' Charlie said. 'There's something special about Mitchell. Know what it is, fellers?'

'Yeah, she's saucy,' one of them said.

'Her mouth's too big,' Charlie said.

'Yeah, it spoils her.'

'She'd be a different person if that mouth was treated. Let's have a look at it.'

I said in a panic, 'Look, he didn't know what he was saying,' and heard my own voice wobbling. 'We're in a hurry. Let's go now.'

'No, it'll only take a minute,' Charlie said, and I saw they were sidling up round us, and I yelled, 'Run, Mike!' and broke clean through and managed to sprint up the lane myself. And Mike managed it, too, only the clot went and tripped. He did it all himself, and went skittering and stumbling almost full length with his arms out in front of him. He didn't go down, but he couldn't right himself, and when I got to the end of the lane and looked back I saw they'd got him up against the wall, and I ran out into the street yelling, 'Help! Police!' and as luck would have it a police car was coming down that very moment and I nearly went into it.

The car braked sharply and the policeman next to the driver said, 'What is it?' And I said, 'It's my friend. He's—' I was going to say, 'He's been set on by a gang,' but I looked back down the lane and saw the gang wasn't there any more. Only Mike was there. He was coming out of the lane a bit slowly. So I said, 'We got lost in there. We couldn't find the way out.' The policeman just looked at me, and waited for Mike, and as he came up he said, 'Are you all right, son?'

Mike was walking slowly and hissing a bit. He opened his mouth to say something, but I got in first and said, 'He fell down. He tripped and fell over in there.' I'd suddenly remembered we weren't supposed to be in the Lanes. We didn't want to go round with the police looking for the gang. We wouldn't see them, but they'd probably see us . . . and decide to see a bit more of us, later.

The policemen were looking at us thoughtfully, and the driver said, 'Where are you trying to get to, then?'

I said, 'George Square.'

He said, 'O.K., hop in. We're going there.'

We got in the back and the car took off, and after a while the chap next to the driver turned round and said, 'What are you doing down the Lanes at night? Don't they tell you about that in school?'

I said, 'I'm sorry. We didn't know where we were.'

He looked at us rather broodingly and said, 'You didn't get in any trouble down there?'

I said, 'No. No trouble,' and after a moment he turned round and faced the front again.

The police didn't want any trouble down the Lanes, either.

They dropped us at our bus stop in George Square, and I had a look at Mike in the light to see what had happened to him. I couldn't see anything. He said he'd protected his face but had collected a couple of digs in the stomach. Also one of them had stamped on his bad foot. He didn't want to talk about it. I remembered he never talked about his foot. He was hardly even looking at me as his bus came up but I could see he was in pain.

I said, 'You want me to see you home, Mike?'

'No, I'm fine.'

'You sure?'

'Sure. See you in the morning,' he said, and got on and

limped inside. I gave him a wave as the bus pulled out but he didn't wave back.

When I got in, my mother said, 'Where've *you* been?'

I said, 'Moggy needed some help, after tea.'

'Who did?'

'Moggy, Mr Morgan, the art master.'

She said, 'Oh,' and tried to hide the special sort of look that came over her face when anything happened at school. She was crazy about our school. She thought it was posh. Moggy's name had been in the papers lately over an exhibition he was helping to organize in town, so this made it even better. She said, 'You could have phoned, or left a note. I didn't know where you were.'

'It just cropped up.'

'And that little foreign boy was here. He brought some stamps. He said you knew he was coming.'

Oh, Gawd! Soldier. He seemed a long time ago, Soldier.

'He was upset you weren't here. He's such a nice boy. He seemed quite hurt.'

'Yeah, well. I couldn't get in touch.'

'Was it something unexpected?'

'Yeah. A bit unexpected. Any supper?' I said.

After supper I got my homework out, and she watched me for a bit out of the corner of her eye.

'Mike not dropping in tonight?' she said, casually.

I said, 'No. Not tonight.'

She didn't say anything, but when a cup of tea came up at nine o'clock, a slice of cake came up with it.

4

Mike wasn't at school next day so I phoned up and went to see him in the evening. Aunt Freda said, 'Hello, Jim. You won't let him get up, will you?' and told me again how he'd fallen off the kerb and hurt his bad leg and had to rest it. I said it sounded nasty and she said it was and asked if I wanted a cup of tea up there. I said I didn't and went up and found him lying on his back, frowning at the ceiling.

I said, 'How's it going?'

He said, '*Hello!*' and broke into his cheerful Charlie smile. 'I was just thinking about you.'

'I thought you looked dead happy.'

'No, I mean about – you know,' he said. I hadn't shut the door properly and he waited till I had and was sitting on the bed. 'Did you mean it – about those chaps starting the fire?'

'Well, it wasn't an accident.'

'Does Moggy think that?'

'Of course. They all want Lepic out of there.'

'Who do?'

'Geezers. Property people, builders, agents. He's the last of the tenants in the block, and he won't sell his lease, and they can't make him, legally. They're trying to persuade him.'

'But why should anyone want Lepic's little place?' Mike said, shaking his head in that peculiar slow way of his that makes you want to lift it off and give it a real shake, like a coconut.

'Because it's in the middle of the building scheme, isn't it?' I said. 'Don't you ever read the papers?'

He said, 'Yeah. Yeah. You know I do.'

I knew he did. I'd seen him. He read the strips, and then the TV programmes, and then the back sports page.

I said, 'Well, he's in the middle, so if they want to go ahead with the building, they're going to have to do it all round him, aren't they? Which will cost them a fortune. Which is why they're *offering* him a fortune to go.'

'Why doesn't he, then?'

'Because he's a nut-case. He doesn't like the idea of anyone putting up a skyscraper on Auldhouses. And they're all getting excited now because of the Market Inquiry.'

'What Market Inquiry?'

'Oh, Gawd!' I said. 'Mike, honest. I mean, you know. You must have heard about that. All this stuff going on about what's to happen to the land after they shift the market.'

'Oh, sure, sure,' Mike said, but he had such a dozy look on his face I knew I'd lost him then. It's a complicated business, anyway. It's more complicated than Auldhouses even, and I didn't explain that before so I better do it now.

It's old, our town. It was a wool town in thirteen hundred and something. The people used to keep sheep and they were experts at weaving, so that various merchants got rich flogging the stuff in Europe.

The best known was a character in the fifteen hundreds called Sir Samuel Turner, who was a clothier – which didn't mean he made clothes; he made cloth. Or rather, the peasants made the cloth and he made the money. He made so much of it, Queen Elizabeth made him a sir, and to show his appreciation he built our school, Turner's. He did that four hundred years ago, and the anniversary was coming up in April. That was why we were doing the mural now.

It was also the reason Moggy was putting on the historical exhibition in town. One of the things about our town, although it's had so much history, hardly any of it shows up today. Since the time Turner made all the money and they were dancing round the Maypole, there hasn't been anything to dance about. Most of the old buildings got knocked down in the Industrial Revolution when the town turned over to making cotton. And when the cotton mills packed in and half the population was thrown out of work, they didn't feel like dancing anyway. So the only real link with the good old days is our school – and Auldhouses.

Auldhouses were built by a Turner, too, although it wasn't Sir Samuel, it was his daughter. He had two daughters, and when he died, one of them married and turned into a Lady, and one of them didn't and turned awkward. This one was called Mary and all the land round Auldhouses was hers (that's the Maryhill housing estate today).

Mary got more awkward as she got older, and the idea of putting up Auldhouses was to show what she thought of men. The homes were supposed to be for single old women. They didn't have to be widows or anything. They just had to stay away from men.

She spent a lot of money on the scheme and had a Board of Trustees to run it, but when they said she was spending too much, she had a row with them and set up another Trust and started spending more. She spent it on some weird things.

I don't know if you know this (we had to do it for the mural), but when they made cloth in those days they had to have a river. They had to have running water. There were impurities in the wool and if you washed it raw, it shrank unevenly and ended up a different shape. They got round this by weaving the stuff very loosely to begin with, like a piece of net or sacking. Then they washed the impurities off in running water, and as the whole thing shrank and tightened they bashed it into shape and bonded the fibres together and got rid of the wrinkles; and that way they ended up with a normal-looking piece of cloth instead of the sack they started with.

The whole job was called 'fulling' (there's more to it than that, but you don't need to bother with it), and it gave everybody a hard time till some genius worked out that if the river already did half the job, it could do the other half as well, the half that had them bashing and swearing.

The way he did it was to stick a wheel in the water, with a contraption on the axle that would make something go up and down whenever the wheel turned. What the genius fixed to the contraption was a series of flat weights that went up and down and did the bashing; so all you had to do was shove the cloth underneath and watch the river go by. This struck everyone as such a fantastically good idea that they fell over themselves getting wheels in the water.

Water-wheels had been going some time by Mary's day but they still cost a lot of money. Mary had a lot of money, so she bought one for her old ladies. (The town already had a few but she didn't want the women using them in case they got chatting to the men.) She also bought weaving-looms and spinning-wheels and a flock of sheep. And because she didn't want the women mixing with the shepherds, she made another gift and got it written in the Trust: an extra piece of land for grazing.

Her general idea was to get the women running all stages of cloth-making so they needn't come in contact with men at all; and also to see they made so much money out of it that they could tell the men to get lost, anyway.

She did all this, and then died, and about a couple of years later, the sheep died, too. Some kind of disease was going round, and as fast as the Trust replaced sheep they kept dying off; till the Trust ran out of funds and the old ladies ran out of patience, and the wheel fell to pieces, and after a while Auldhouses did, too.

By the seventeen hundreds the ruins were being used as slaughter-houses (which is how the market sprang up round there), and it wasn't till Victorian times that things started looking up again. That was when a London designer called William Morris happened to visit Auldhouses, and he said it was a shame historic buildings should be such an eyesore, and they ought to be rebuilt, with the orginal materials.

He got various people to see it his way, and the council told him to go ahead and do it, which he did. But half way through, they all realized they'd run into a snag.

Under the terms of the Trust, the property could only be used for the original purpose, and the town already had an old-people's home – it had been put up by some other charity not long before. Morris hated to see his big idea going to waste, so he looked into Mary's story and found out about the spinning and weaving (which he was crazy about himself, anyway, together with all kinds of other arts and crafts), and he came up with a new idea.

He said it would be in the spirit of Mary Turner's wishes if Auldhouses became a 'community of hand-workers'. What he meant was they ought to turn the place over to arts and crafts.

The council said O.K., but when you want to change a Trust you have to get legal permission, and in this case it meant Parliament's. Morris had friends in Parliament and he got them to say O.K., too. But they wrote a couple of things into the Trust which caused all the headaches later on.

They said because the buildings were part of a charity, not much rent could be charged for them. And because the rent was low (they said how low it had to be) the tenants had to be given long leases so nobody could throw them out.

Morris wasn't interested in the rent, and neither was the council (the town was such a dump, nobody was queuing to pay rent, anyway). So they put various craftsmen in the houses and forgot the whole thing – till just about twenty years ago, when the town started changing.

New factories had been going up for some time, and new people had moved in; and where you get that, you also get new housing and shops and schools and hospitals and so on, so that in no time the shape of the place changed. One result was that while the market and Auldhouses used to be on the outskirts of town, they were in the middle now. And because nobody planned it that way, fantastic traffic jams built up.

To sort the problem out, the council decided to shift the market. But that led to arguments about what to do with the space, and since they didn't want the same mess a few years later, they decided to have a public inquiry to discuss the various schemes.

One scheme was to turn it into public gardens and playing fields – and this was backed by the governors of our school, because we were short of space. And another was to make it the new town centre – and this was backed by the builders because it would cost a ton of money and they'd all be laughing.

This idea had brought a lot of developers forward, with fantastic plans. They said they'd lay out a square and a new roadway and underground car-parks, and all around they'd build groups of skyscrapers and shopping arcades and plazas.

The only snag with this scheme was that the market area wasn't big enough. To do the job properly they'd have to knock down the Lanes – which was a good idea anyway, and nobody objected – except that between the Lanes and the market area there was Auldhouses. And they couldn't knock Auldhouses down.

At least, they couldn't if anyone was in them. If nobody was in them, they probably could. They'd have to go to Parliament and put up an argument; but they'd already said in the newspaper what the argument was, and it wasn't bad.

They said it was crazy to block the needs of a townful of people just because an old woman, dead for centuries, had other ideas. Her ideas hadn't been followed, anyway. Her almshouses weren't needed so they'd been turned into workshops. And now the workshops weren't needed, and they were empty and useless and in everyone's way.

It was such a good argument, most people were sure they'd get away with it. Some of the people were so sure, they'd been going around buying up slum property in the Lanes, with the idea of selling it at a fantastic profit to the characters who would have to put skyscrapers there.

The only thing was, there wouldn't be any skyscrapers unless everyone left Auldhouses. And not everyone was going to leave. Lepic wasn't.

This is what I was trying to tell Mike, and I only hope you got it, too; because it was a drag putting it down, and unless you got it you're not going to understand how Moggy got himself in the position of having his head bashed in, or how Mike and Soldier and I got in the position with him.

5

It was Friday I went into all that with Mike, so we didn't have school till Monday, and Monday was art. His foot was O.K. now, so he stood next to me at the mural, groaning as usual – except not as much. He didn't have his mind on his work and kept trying to catch Moggy's eye. Only Moggy didn't have his mind on his work, either, and kept out the way.

Mike caught him as he drifted round once, and pretended he needed advice, but Moggy gave it quickly and didn't hang around.

'What's up with him?' Mike said, worried.

'He's embarrassed about us. Leave him alone.'

'Yeah, well, I'm going to see him at break,' Mike said.

'He won't want to see you.'

'He doesn't have to be embarrassed,' Mike said.

He didn't have any luck at break, though. I thought I hadn't been wrong: Moggy was embarrassed. He just said he was in a hurry and had to dash off.

'Where to?'

'To grab a cup of coffee in the staff room,' Mike said weakly.

'Yeah. Well. I told you. He doesn't want to see you. He's worried.'

'He doesn't have to worry by himself,' Mike said.

He started worrying for him. He worried all through French, which isn't his best subject. (Apart from art, I don't know what is.) In French we were on Book Four, about this French family that keeps going away every weekend and buying things. All the stuff they buy seems to be the wrong size or the wrong colour or too dear. They'd spent a fortune on this useless gear all through Book Four.

Anyway, they were at a hotel again this week, complaining as usual, and they'd already found out all the things wrong with it, and they were asking about the service in the restaurant, and Mike had been having a hard time pronouncing the *maître* in *maître d'hotel*, which is what they call the head waiter.

But they got through with that and started ordering dinner, so Mike was let off the hook and looked out the window instead and got back to worrying about Moggy; and Fleming (the twit who takes us for French) didn't notice for a bit because he's keen on food and had livened up as soon as they got on the menu.

We went through the usual nonsense with nobody in the rotten family being able to make up his mind what to eat. Their nit of a kid François asked the waiter the name of every soup in the hotel before he said he'd have grapefruit, and I'm only surprised the waiter didn't kick his head in for him.

Then they finished with that, and his pest of a sister Monique, who's such a genius at housekeeping, had to look at the windows and say they were dirty and needed a wash. Fleming has this weird habit of pointing both hands at anything that happens to be mentioned, as if he's walking in his sleep, and when *fenêtre*, window, came up, he did it at the window; and for the first time noticed Mike sitting there looking out of it, so he yelled, 'Mitchell!'

'Yes, sir?' Mike said, with a jump.

'Try and pretend you're with us, Mitchell,' Fleming said. 'What was the last thing we read?'

Mike hadn't read it so he didn't know, but he has this trick of repeating what he just heard, so he said, 'It's dirty and needs a wash.'

'What does?' Fleming said.

'Er,' Mike said.

'Well, read it, boy. Right there in the book, page 98, line 6.'

Mike had a look at page 98, line 6 and found *fenêtre*, only he was still bugged over *maître*, so he said it was the head waiter that was dirty and needed the wash, and Fleming nearly went up the wall. What made it worse, everybody practically passed out laughing, and Fleming thought they were laughing at him and flew in a temper, and he sat down and wrote Mike a note to take to the Head.

This was pretty serious. Mike didn't want to see the Cobbler again. He said, 'I'm sorry, sir. I didn't think for a minute. I've got a headache.'

'You will have,' Fleming said. 'Go on. Hand it in right away.'

Mike didn't say anything. He just uncoiled out of his seat and took the note and went and I didn't see him again all morning. I didn't see him in the afternoon, either, but that was because Monday afternoon was football and he didn't do it.

It was a hassle at our school, football. The school field was only for the younger kids. The rest of us had to go miles out to this other field at Rennisham. The school bus ran out there, only the driver always took off early – he lived at Rennisham – so if you missed it, you'd had it. You had to hang about waiting for two other buses, and one of them only ran every hour.

Parents had complained about it for years, which was why the school was after the market area as new playing fields. The thing about our school is, it changed into a different kind of school a few years back. It used to be private, with fee-paying boarders, but when it became a Direct Grant school (which meant the Government gave the money to run it directly to the Board of Governors), they had to get rid of the boarders.

Nobody had to pay now, but you could only get in if you passed the exam. At least, that was the idea. Mike didn't have to pass it, but I already said why; and Soldier didn't, either, because he was a foreigner, and they got him in under some special rule because his father was a professor.

When they got the money from the Government they had to agree to take in a lot more kids, which meant more class-rooms and also the new science block, out in the grounds, so the playing fields got chewed up, which is why we had to go to Rennisham.

Anyway, for the same reason the swine who drove the bus was always early taking off, he was always late turning up to take us back, so I never got home before six. I rang Mike up when I got back, and his Mum answered and said he hadn't come in yet.

I said, 'Where from?'

'School, I suppose. He had a job to do.'

'Oh.'

'Didn't you know about it?'

'Yeah. I suppose so, I forgot.' I said.

I wondered what this was about and waited for him to call back. He hadn't called by eight, so I called him.

He said, 'Oh, hello.'

I said, 'Where you been?'

'Oh, well. You know.'

'What? The Cobbler?'

'No, no. The other thing.'

'What other thing?'

'Yeah, well,' Mike said, so I knew his Mum was there.

'You want me to come round?' I said. His voice was pretty dead-beat. I could hardly hear it.

'Not really.'

'Here, are you all right, Mike?'

'See you in the morning, then,' he said, and there was a

click, and I said, 'Hello,' but he'd hung up, and I looked at the phone in my hand and slowly put it down. I couldn't go round if he didn't want me to. Something was wrong, though.

I was still worrying about it in bed. I wondered if I ought to go round there anyway – the short way, up the drain-pipe to his room. He'd done the same with me a few times. It was raining outside, though, and while I was thinking about it I fell asleep.

Mike is such a worrier, he always worries he'll be late for school so he gets there dead early. I thought I better get there early, too, and found him mooching about just looking at the ground. He told me what he'd been up to last night.

He'd been to see Moggy in the afternoon. He just hung around the art room till the class there was finished, and caught Moggy as he came out. Moggy tried to put him off again, but Mike just stuck with him and said he wanted to help and he'd do anything he could.

Moggy said there was nothing anyone could do. He was supposed to have the one-man show Easter week, but there was no hope of the place being ready. For a month after that Lepic was having an exhibition for a firm that made art supplies, and after that he had a list of shows for other artists. He'd given Moggy the only week he had available for about a year.

'Well, that's it, then,' I said.

'Yeah. It is. I thought something could still be done about it, but it can't. It isn't just the muck on the floor and the wall-sacking and the windows and that. The thing is, the walls are original – there's still the old wood and stones behind the plaster, and they've got to be redone. The fire burnt the wood and you can pull the stones out. I could even see right through'.

'I couldn't. It was dark.'

'No, well, he's got the electricity back now. I had a good look at it.'

'You what?'

He'd been back. That's why he'd been late getting home. He hadn't told Moggy. He'd just gone. He found the front had been boarded up so he went round the back and got in through a window, and switched the light on and had a look at it. He hadn't even see Lepic. He hadn't seen anybody – except he'd gone and seen the mob.

They must have noticed the light through the cracks in the boarding at the front, and they were waiting for him at the end of the alley when he came out. Only there's two ways out of the alley, and he went pelting out the other end. They went after him, but he didn't trip this time and he has a good turn of speed. He nipped out through the market and zig-zagged through the various sections and managed to jump on a bus in Hill Street, at the other side.

He thought they'd tailed him, though. He'd spotted an orange Volkswagen following the bus. It slowed when the bus slowed and didn't try to overtake. He hadn't got off at his normal stop. He went past and jumped off while the bus was still moving, and ran down a side street, so the Volkswagen would have to make a U-turn in the main road to follow. He didn't know if it did or not. He saw a car's lights swing into the street soon after, but he didn't hang around to see what kind of car. He'd put me off going round there in case they were still cruising.

I said, 'Honest, Mike. You need your head examined. Why'd you want to go round there alone?'

'Who else could I have gone with? You weren't around. I mean, I wouldn't, anyway. I didn't want to drag you in it again. I thought if I could do it all myself, then maybe . . .' he said drearily. 'Well, that's it.'

'So long as that's all.'

'Yeah. Well. It isn't,' Mike said.

'There's something else?'

'The Cobbler, you see.'

'What did he say?'

'I didn't see him.'

'He wasn't there?'

'I don't know,' Mike said. 'I never went.'

'*You what?*'

'Yeah. I know,' Mike said, miserably.

'Mike, Gawd. That's serious!'

'Well, I thought if I was going to get kicked out anyway, I could do without any more of his comments.'

'But Mike –'

'I know, I know,' Mike said. 'It's how I felt then. I been thinking about it since. I mean, it wasn't *certain* I was going to get kicked out. Not then, it wasn't. It is now. Unless Fleming forgets or something,' he said hopelessly.

He knew Fleming wouldn't forget. Fleming couldn't forget. When they give you a note, you get your name written in a book. I'd seen Fleming do it. Then when the note comes back, whatever the Cobbler's written on it goes in the book, too. They take it into account when they work out the end-of-term reports.

It's lousy to get a note, anyway, but to get one and not hand it in is murder. We had French Mondays and Wednesdays. On Wednesday Fleming was going to open the book and then it was curtains for Mike. The thing is, Mike couldn't just go and hand in the note now, anyway. The notes are dated, so the Cobbler would ask him why he hadn't done it before. Either way, he was in a tough position.

We were going through the possibilities when Soldier showed up. He's an early bird, too. I started telling him to get lost, but Mike is always good with him, and he said, 'Hi, Soldier.'

41

'Hi,' Soldier said, and looked at him. 'Is something wrong?' he asked.

Mike started telling him, and Soldier shook his head. 'It's not good, it's not good,' he said. He's like a little old man, and he's still got this foreign accent. 'Perhaps we change the date?' he said.

We hadn't thought of that, so Mike got out the note and gloomily had a look at it. He'd already steamed the envelope open at home. I had a look at it with him, and I saw right away it was no use.

Fleming doesn't do his figures like anyone else. He does these Roman numerals. Yesterday's date was March 8th, so he'd put it iii/viii. To make the 8 into a 9 you'd have to alter viii to ix, which was pretty near impossible.

While I was at it, I read what he'd written, and saw why Mike was so gloomy. Fleming had told the Cobbler all the business about the head waiter needing the wash, and he ended up, 'Mitchell's new role as class comedian, in addition to his general uselessness at this school, seems to me to call for the strongest measures.'

'H'm,' Soldier said, looking at it, too. 'We can't alter the date, anyway. Maybe we have to try something bigger. You have some of the Cobbler's writing?'

'Eh?' Mike said.

I got the point. Soldier had told me about it before. When they came to England, his family had to escape from this other country, and his old man had forged various papers. To copy another person's handwriting, you have to turn the paper round and copy it upside down and back to front: that way you don't get any of your own style in, and it comes out not too bad.

'Well, I don't know,' Mike said, when he got the point.

'You must have some of his writing,' Soldier said. 'On a report, say.'

'I suppose I must have,' Mike said, a bit uneasily.

Most of the school had turned up by this time, and whistles were blowing, so we dropped it and agreed we'd go back with Mike after school and have a look at his reports.

And after school, we did. Mike was still a bit uneasy, and when we got up to his room we found out why. His reports had been so terrible, he'd just thrown most of them away. The only one he'd kept was the best, and all the Cobbler had written on the bottom of it was, 'A *very slight improvement.*'

'Yes, well that's no good,' Soldier said.

'No.' It wasn't. Whatever nutty thing the Cobbler might say, he wasn't likely to say that Mike's turning into the class comedian was any improvement.

'Is there anything else?' Soldier said.

'There's that stinking letter about kicking me out if I don't do better,' Mike said miserably. 'But that's no good.'

'Let's have a look at it,' Soldier said.

We all had a look at it. It was to his mother, and it certainly was a stinker. The Cobbler said Mike didn't seem able to benefit from the school, and contributed nothing to it himself, and he ended up, 'I have spoken to him and I hope have made clear that, apart from the need to keep up our own standards, he would be happier himself at a school where less was demanded of him, and that therefore unless some marked improvement takes place I will reluctantly have to inform the school Secretary that there will be no need to enter his name for the next school year.'

'Yeah, Really useless,' I said.

'I don't know,' Soldier said.

'How d'you mean?'

'Well . . .' He'd started doodling. He'd got a bit of paper and was writing out a few words from the beginning and the end of what the Cobbler had written, with a dash in between. He wrote it out a couple of times, and then turned the

Cobbler's letter upside down and copied out the words he wanted in the Cobbler's own handwriting. When he'd got it really right, he did the whole thing on the back of Fleming's note, and added the Cobbler's initials.

'How about that?' he said.

'Crikey!' Mike said. He read it again and looked at Soldier as if he was a magician. 'It's fantastic,' he said.

The words Soldier had picked out from the Cobbler's note and transferred to the back of Fleming's read:

'I have spoken to him – no need to enter his name. – W.J.C.'

'Worth a try, isn't it?' Soldier said.

French was Wednesday, and that was next day. Mike was looking a bit weird when he went in. He shook hands with me in the doorway. We didn't sit next to each other in French. He was over by the window, near Nixon.

Fleming was in a bad temper when he came in. He had a cold and was blowing his nose. He was still blowing it when he sat down, and he opened the book with his other hand.

'Who have we got here?' he said.

A creep called Wrigley, who sits at the front and tells everyone everything, told him who we were.

'Ah. A treat,' Fleming said. 'Mitchell!'

'Yes, sir?' Mike said.

'The sight of your name in the book gives me reason to believe,' Fleming said, polishing off his pink snout, 'that you will have a little message for me from the Head.'

'Oh. Yes, sir,' Mike said, and started looking through all his pockets as if he didn't know which one it was in. His lips were dry, and he was licking them as he went up to the table with the envelope.

The envelope had been a bit of a problem. What the Cobbler usually does, he crosses out his own name on the front and puts in the name of whatever master it has to go to, and sticks it up again with a bit of tape. We didn't have Fleming's name in his writing, so Soldier had just crossed it out and left it at that. We'd taped it up, though.

Fleming looked at the envelope, still wriggling his nose and sniffing, and he opened it, and took out his own note and read it, and then turned it over and read the Cobbler's: that is, Soldier's. He looked at it for several seconds while Mike stood there trembling, then he tore it up and threw it in the basket, and said, 'Very good, Mitchell. Go and sit down.'

Mike went and sat down, and I saw his white face looking at me across the room, and I winked at him.

Fleming didn't see it. He was busy crossing Mike's name out of the book.

I don't know if it was right, any of this. I don't know if it was right trying to keep Mike at the school, either. Maybe he would have been better off somewhere else. But he wouldn't have been 'happier' as the Cobbler and the rest said. That was a load of tripe. He was happier sticking with me. He'd be worried and anxious elsewhere – at least right now. Later it might be different. And anyway, he was learning a bit and trying his best.

He was no genius, but who was? The Cobbler wasn't. He didn't teach or anything. He only had to run the place – and he made a mess of that. There were always snarl-ups about the timetable, and new equipment that wasn't there on time, and new textbooks that weren't, either. And more than half the school still had to go out to flaming Rennisham every week because he hadn't managed anything better in the way of playing fields. If it came to making 'contributions' I could think of someone who could start showing 'marked improvement' himself.

I wasn't going round thinking this all the time, and wondering if it was right or wrong. I mean, I hardly thought about it at all. But I knew it couldn't be too way-out to give Mike a shove when he needed it, and I knew that because he was like that himself. It was the part of him I liked best, really.

6

I already said, if Mike stuck to you, he really stuck, and it got like that with him and Moggy. Of course it started when Moggy threw him the compliment about his instinct, because Mike was a bit short of compliments at the time. But it would have happened anyway after the bad luck with the fire. Mike knew all about bad luck himself.

After that, you couldn't say anthing without him bringing Moggy into it. Moggy couldn't do anything wrong. If he fell over his feet and landed on his nose, Mike would have said how well he did it. Round about then he started running errands for Moggy. They were mainly to do with the historical exhibition. The exhibition had started with the mural, too, and I see I haven't put too much about it, so I better do it now.

When you do a mural, you have to start with a 'key'. It's the original picture, but done much smaller. Moggy had done this. In fact, he'd done several. Our class only had one section. The whole thing was going round the school hall, and we had the end wall.

What he'd done, he'd marked up the pictures into numbered squares, and transferred the pencilled squares to the big hardboard panels that we had to do the mural on. We'd each been given a block of numbers and we had to copy whatever was in 'our' squares from the small pictures to the hardboard. It was like painting by numbers, but trickier, because we were working in teams and had to get everything matching.

The mural wasn't only about the school. It covered the

whole history of the town, and before he'd worked it out, Moggy had done a lot of research. He'd travelled all over the county finding costumes, furniture, tools and so on. And he got so excited he went to see the mayor and told him all the stuff I put earlier (about how the school's anniversary was really the town's and it was time they had something to dance about).

The mayor liked the idea and put it to the council, and they decided they wouldn't have just one exhibition but two – in the town hall itself, with big displays of the way people used to live, and one in the county library for things like books and pictures and documents.

They voted money for the scheme and gave Moggy an assistant; only the assistant turned out to be a dozy town-hall clerk who was permanently tired, so it ended up with Moggy doing most of the running himself. Until Mike showed up, wagging his ears and flapping his paws and begging to help, and Moggy let him do some of the running for him.

By that time he'd done a lot himself. The thing had been going for months. The library exhibition was easiest and he'd fixed most of that. In fact he'd already done an article on it for the school magazine. The magazine comes out twice a year, Christmas and Easter, and we get it the week before we break up. The Easter one hadn't come from the printers yet, but Moggy already had a proof copy, and he showed it to Mike, and I think you'd better read the next bit carefully, because it's important.

The article Moggy wrote was about how he'd gone around finding the pictures and documents for the library exhibition. The county library had plenty of material itself; only a lot of it was stuck away in the basement, and not easy to get at.

Moggy had to blow the dust off piles of old rubbish to find what he wanted. He found some great things. In one pile he found a brown-paper parcel that hadn't been opened since it was put there in 1907. It was a load of old prints and papers, bought from a bookseller called Bickersley, and they knew the date because his invoice was still inside. It said Bickersley had bought the stuff at an auction in York and had sold it to the library for £1.

There were some useful old prints that showed buildings knocked down long ago, and the papers were even more useful – one of them a surveyor's report that went into every constructional detail about one of the buildings. But the most useful document of all was from a different period entirely. It was a stiffish sheet of parchment, folded over four times, and when they got it in the light they found Mary Turner's signature on it, and it turned out to be an addition to her Trust Deed for Auldhouses.

This caused a terrific lot of excitement because there were no documents at all about the Turners, and various university people came to examine it, and said it was quite authentic and apparently the extra Trust that Mary Turner had made when she gave the grazing land to her old ladies.

Moggy was naturally very chuffed about this and he took a picture of it, and another one of the chief librarian holding it up and grinning like a maniac, and he printed both photos with his article, and that's how it all started. I mean, that's how he came to get his head bashed in.

All I can put now is what Mike told me, because at that time I hadn't seen the magazine. Apart from Moggy, Mike was the only one in the school who had seen it. The proof copy was a bit smudgy, but the picture showed clearly enough what was written in the document.

The bit that mattered said:

I do give and attach to the Mary Turner Almshouses in perpetuity alle that parcell of land knowne as Brooke Meddowes consisting of twenty-five acres together with the brydge from the Brooke Dribbel going north towards Hedgehogg Hille and bounded on the east by Alle-Hallowes Churche and on the west by Martin Fyldes Fullers Fields.

Mike read this and he started nodding and he said, 'Yeah, that's a funny thing. I always thought it looked like one myself.' And Moggy said, 'What?' And Mike said, 'A hedgehog.' And Moggy said, 'What are you talking about, Mitchell?'

So Mike told him. He said while he was lying in hospital all that year with his leg he used to look across to the hill opposite, and if you held your head some funny way it looked like a hedgehog.

Moggy looked at him for a bit, and he said, 'Take me to see it, Mitchell. Let me see it from where you saw it.' So they took a bus to the hospital and went up to the roof and had a look from there.

By this time Mike was feeling a fool, and he said, 'Look, Mr Morgan. It was a dopey idea of mine. The thing looks like a hedgehog because of all the TV aerials. And anyway, you've got to hold your head like this.'

They both of them started holding their heads sideways, and Moggy said in a funny voice, 'Dammit, it is a hedgehog. Do you know what that place is, Mitchell?'

Mike said, 'Yeah, it's the Maryhill housing estate.'

'Exactly, *Mary*hill. It's called after Mary Turner. That was her land.'

'Yeah, well, I'm sorry,' Mike said.

'Don't be sorry! Your instinct is working again, Mitchell.'

'Eh?' Mike said.

'Mm. Only who's Martin Fyldes, and where are his fuller's fields? Also, where's All Hallows Church?'

'There isn't one,' Mike said. Moggy came from London and didn't know the area too well. 'There's an All Hallows at Lyncham, out in the country.'

'But there might have been,' Moggy said. 'Also where's the Dribble brook?'

'The Dribble's out in the country, too,' Mike said. 'It's at Drifford.'

'But where does it go?'

'It doesn't go anywhere,' Mike said.

'Brooks must go somewhere. You're sure it doesn't go into the Rush?' The Rush is the town river.

'Positive,' Mike said. 'It stops at Drifford. It goes in a kind of water company thing there.'

'But did it always? You see? That's the point,' Moggy said.

Mike didn't get the point, but he nodded away, and Moggy didn't say anything for about twenty minutes. He just had a look all around. You get a good view up there. You can see the Lanes, and Auldhouses, and behind Auldhouses, the market, and behind that Hill Street, and at the top of it, Maryhill. That's what Moggy was looking at, and when he'd finished he turned round and had a look at Mike, and his face was white.

He said, 'Do you know what I think you've just gone and done, Mitchell?'

'What's that?' Mike said.

'I think you've just gone and created the new town plan,' Moggy said.

We knew what he meant the following week. The whole town did. We'd got our magazines by then, anyway; but Moggy had done another article – a real bomber, for the newspaper. He hadn't wasted any time. He'd done a lot more research. What he found out was this:

The Dribble used to run into the Rush. It had cut across the back of Auldhouses. It had become polluted over a century ago because of the rubbish the slaughter-houses threw in it, so the Water Board had stopped it. They'd stopped it just outside Drifford, and the water was used for the town supply now.

There had been a church at All Hallows to the east of Auldhouses, and the slaughter-houses had put paid to that, too. There was such a stink round there, most of the people moved away, and several years later the disused church had been turned into a warehouse. The warehouse itself had fallen into ruins and had been knocked down in 1844.

He didn't know where 'Martin Fyldes Fullers Fieldes' were, but he didn't need to know. He had three of the boundaries of 'that parcell of land knowne as Brooke Meddowes consisting of twenty-five acres.'

One of them was the line of the Dribble (behind Auldhouses); another was the site of All Hallows (east of Auldhouses); the third was the Maryhill estate (north of Auldhouses). All he had to do was take a surveyor there and set him going inside the three lines to see what twenty-five acres would give you.

The surveyor took one look at it, and hardly needed to measure. But he measured, anyway. He just measured up the market. It went exactly twenty acres; and that's what had happened to the old ladies' grazing land. Over the centuries the disused land had *become* the market area.

Once you knew that, a lot of other things became clear. Or, the way Moggy put it in the paper, 'an intelligent reading of the document illuminates much of Mary Turner's intention.'

If she'd built a water-wheel for her old ladies, she must have had water near by. And if she'd given them pasturage to stop them chatting up the town' shepherds, that must have been near by, too. In fact, from Moggy's reconstructed drawing, the whole thing had been one big field, with the Dribble running through it ('Brooke Meddowes'). The almshouses had been on one side of the brook, and the grazing on the other, with the 'brydge' in between.

The water-wheel wasn't mentioned in the document, so that must have been the subject of some other Trust Deed. In fact, Moggy worked out quite a good theory for this. He said the building of the expensive water-wheel might have led to Mary's quarrel with the original Board of Trustees.

And he wrote, 'If so, we may be very thankful, for it impelled Mary Turner to place her affairs, and her documents, in other, and safer, hands – hence the extraordinary preservation over the years of this Trust Deed. As is well known, no Trust Deeds exist either for Turner's School or Auldhouses, and both of these were undoubtedly in the same hands.'

He made another point. He said because the other Deeds had vanished, nobody knew who the original Trustees were. In the case of the school, it had become largely traditional, 'and we may respect tradition'. And in the case of Auldhouses it wasn't important, because the council had taken over responsibility when Morris had got busy in the last century, and Parliament had told them what they could and couldn't do.

'But here for the first time we are presented with a Board of Trustees indisputably appointed by Mary Turner. And today, as four hundred years ago, they have full authority to interpret her wishes. Mary Turner gave the land. The Trustees are to say what is to be done with it.'

The Trustees, as laid down by Mary in the Deed, were, 'the High Master of Sir Samuel Turner's Grammar Schoole; the Chiefe of the Gouvernours of the Same; the Rectoure of Thys Paryshe; and the Successours to Samuel Fogge Esquyre.'

Nobody knew who Fogge Esquyre was, but the rest were still going. The 'High Master' was the Cobbler; the 'Chiefe of the Gouvernours' was Nixon's old man, Dr Nixon. And the

Rectoure was the Rector – who was also chairman of our Playing Fields Committee.

It didn't look as if there'd be any skyscrapers going up in the market area. But in case anyone still had any doubts, Moggy rubbed it in.

'Should the Council still feel the necessity of going through with the farce of holding a Market Inquiry,' he wrote, 'I give warning that I will be there, with the evidence. Meanwhile, when the County Library exhibition opens, any concerned citizen may freely go and inspect that evidence for himself.'

The day afterwards, a couple of citizens were so concerned, they didn't even bother waiting for the exhibition to open. They went and inspected the evidence at about two o'clock in the morning. They went in through a window, and they went out the same way, and the evidence went out with them. It wasn't there in the morning.

I had a glimpse at the newspaper on the way to school. The big black headline said DEED STOLEN – LIBRARY BREAK-IN, and farther down there was more black type. It said, 'It is understood that grave doubts already existed as to the authenticity of the document. Now, with apparently no legally-attested copy, it is doubtful if the "evidence" can be submitted to the Inquiry at all.'

I didn't have time to read any more. It was our last morning at school, and I was late. When I got there, they were all talking about it.

It was a lousy morning, anyway. In the middle of it we got our reports, and it only needed one look at Mike to see what he'd got in his.

He'd got the boot.

7

He'd been expecting it for months – dreading it, really – but he still looked as if he was going to be sick. His mouth was trembling and he kept swallowing. I didn't know what to say to him at break. I just gave him a nudge. A few other characters came up and gave him one, too.

It was such a lousy deal. He'd been running himself dizzy lately, for the rotten school and the exhibition. Then there'd been the other business – his instinct and 'Hedgehogg Hille' – that had bucked him up. Now everything had fallen in, all at once.

School packed in after lunch, but he didn't want to face his mother yet, so we walked for a bit.

I said awkwardly, 'Dammit, Mike. It's not the end of the world.'

'Oh, sure.'

'I mean. You know. We'll see each other as much as ever.'

'Sure, sure.'

He knew we wouldn't, and so did I, so I dropped that. I said, 'You don't feel like mentioning it to Moggy, then?' We'd had a word about it at lunch.

'Not really.'

'I mean, you helped *him*. It wouldn't hurt him, would it? He doesn't want you to get the boot.'

'Well. You know. He's got his own worries.'

'It isn't July yet, though.'

They weren't kicking him out till July. They can't kick you out just like that. They just said he wasn't down for the next school year. I don't know if it was better or worse for him, coming back after Easter and drearily hanging on for three months. He knew that when the school year finished he was finished with it. And everybody else knew.

He said, 'Well, I'll think about it.'

'You'll be seeing him, anyway, will you – Moggy?'

'Oh, sure. There's things still to do. That is – I suppose so. I don't know now.'

I said, 'Of course you will. This doesn't change anything. You been working with him.' They'd done a lot of the work at Moggy's place. He wasn't married, Moggy. He had digs in Waterloo Street. 'Mention it to him, Mike. It can't do any harm.'

'Yeah, O.K.,' Mike said. But I knew from his tone of voice that he wouldn't.

I thought somebody had better mention it. I thought I'd better. I couldn't think what number Waterloo Street he lived, though. I tried to think of some way of asking Mike, without letting him know why. Just before we peeled off, I said, 'What's Moggy's landlady called?'

'Moggy's landlady? Mrs Cripps. Why?'

'Cripps, that's it. I knew it was something like chips. I was just thinking of a bag of chips,' I said.

As a joke, it was so weak it could hardly stand up, and I don't know what I'd have said if it was some other name. But he didn't catch on, so that was all right, and I went home and got out the phone book, and found her there, *Cripps, Ada, 74 Waterloo Street*; and that was all right, too.

He said, 'You want to do what?'

I said, 'I want to come and see you, Mr Morgan. If you're not busy.'

'Well, I am. Is it important?'

'Yes.'

'Oh.' He sounded scrambled. It had taken him some time

56

to get to the phone. He said, 'Who d'you say you are – Woolcott?'

'That's right, Mr Morgan.'

'Oh, Woolcott. You're a friend of Mitchell's.'

'Yeah, that's what I want to talk about.'

'Goddam it!' he said. He didn't say it to me. He seemed to have dropped something. I thought it was the phone for a while, because it went bumping about, but apparently it wasn't, because he said he'd have to wash it now.

'It's all these things in my hands, you see,' he said.

'I see,' I said.

You had to put up with a lot from him. He seemed to think I could see him.

'Well, all right, Woolcott,' he said impatiently. 'But make it snappy. I've got to be out in half an hour. Have you got the address?'

'I've got it.'

'Mrs Cripps will let you in. But don't go away if I'm not there. O.K.?'

'O.K.'

'Because I am there. You got that?'

'Yeah. I think so,' I said.

I wasn't sure if he was all there any of the time, but I didn't argue the point. I just hung up and got moving.

His Mrs Cripps let me in and said, 'It's up three flights, dear, top floor. You don't have to knock. I'll buzz him for you. Don't go away if he's not there.'

'No, all right.'

'Because he is,' she said.

H'm. A whole houseful of them. I went up. Moggy seemed to live in the attic. The ceiling sloped even in the passage. There were two doors, and I waited for a bit, but nothing happened, so I tried them. One was a cupboard. I put my ear to the other one and heard water running somewhere. Moggy still seemed to be washing it, whatever it was.

While I was listening I heard the door being unlocked and got my ear away just in time. The door opened and Moggy was standing there in a pair of swimming trunks. That's all he had on. His hands were wet.

'Come in, Woolcott, come in. It's an absolutely beauty,' he said.

'Eh?'

'An absolute cracker. A corker. A pippin. If this doesn't send them round the twist, I don't know what will. You want a drink of anything?'

'No, thanks. I wanted to talk about –'

'Well, sit down, Woolcott, sit down,' he said.

He'd already sat down himself. He was grinning away, quite relaxed. He didn't seem to be in a tearing hurry to go anywhere. I had a quick look round the place. It was the most terrible mess. He had a big skylight on top, so he could do his painting, and he had paintings everywhere. They were hanging about, cock-eyed, on the walls. There was one with a tin can, and I saw what Mike meant about the anchor. He seemed to have decided against the anchor. The little anchor with a rope through it was on a big table jammed up against the window with an incredible pile of other junk; he had tubes of paint and jars of brushes and little piles of useless things like cotton reels and old motor horns. He stuck all this gear on his pictures, and a few dozen of the crazy pictures were stacked all round the room, leaning against the walls.

I took my eyes off it, and said, 'It's about Mitchell, you see.'

'Mitchell. Yes. You're friends, aren't you?'

'Cousins, actually.'

'Cousins, heh? Well, well. H'm,' Moggy said.

He wasn't actually grinning at me. There was a little door at the far end of the room, and the sound of water was coming from there. He seemed to be grinning at that. He was rubbing his nose at the same time and almost coming out with a little 'Tee-hee' under his breath.

I said, a bit desperately, 'The thing is, he's got the – He's been dismissed from the school.'

'Dismissed from the school? Who has?'

'Mike has. Mitchell!' I said, practically yelping at him. I thought a dip in the bath next door might help him. He was so mixed up in whatever private joke he'd got going, he seemed hardly aware I was there at all. What I'd just said shifted the grin off his face, though.

He said, 'Why?'

I said, 'Well. They say his work's not up to it.'

'Mitchell's work? Why, he's a brilliant boy.'

'Yeah. Well,' I said. I had to pick my words carefully. He's a nut, Moggy, but I didn't want to put him off. 'In certain subjects, he isn't so brilliant. But it's not his fault. He was in hospital for a year, and he lost time, and he hasn't settled down yet. But he's trying. I mean – he's a good bloke, Mike. You know that.'

'He's an excellent bloke,' Moggy said. 'I never heard such nonsense.'

'The thing is, he can't do sports, because of his leg. And since he can't contribute in *that* way, and he's a bit slow in some others – I mean, not that it's his fault. But they say –'

'Who says?'

'The Cob – Mr Cobbridge does. He's the one who sacked him, you see. So I was wondering if you could –'

'H'm.'

'– put in a word for him. Get him a bit more time.'

'Time,' Moggy said, and looked at his watch. 'One minute.'

He really was a nut. He was worried about Mike, I could see that, but he was more worried by whatever else he'd got on his mind. I didn't seem to be getting through to him.

I said, 'Mr Morgan. Could you go and see Mr Cobbridge, please? What I was thinking – if you could persuade him Mike really did have something to contribute to the school, something they might have overlooked – you know, just to try and get him another year. I mean, he *is* trying. And it really isn't fair. And I know you think he's got *something*.'

'I doubt if I could sway Mr Cobbridge,' Moggy said, still looking at his watch.

'*Yeah, well – you could try, couldn't you!*' I said.

I practically shouted it at him, I was so angry. I'd suddenly thought of old Mike, panting all over town for him, and too shy to ask anything for himself in case he added to Moggy's troubles; and here Moggy was, looking at his watch and counting off minutes when Mike's whole future was at stake. Well – I mean, blow his future. He was flaming unhappy now.

'Why couldn't you?' I said.

Moggy looked at me, a bit surprised. He said mildly, 'You see, I don't know if you understand, but an art master –' and a buzzer went off suddenly, and he stopped. I thought it was his Mrs Cripps buzzing him, but it wasn't. He got up and went in the room where the water was running, and turned it off, and a few seconds later I heard him cackling again, and he called out, 'Come here.'

I went in and found a little room with a red light on. It was a photographic darkroom. He'd got a lot of gear in there, and two big sinks. The tap had been running in one of them, and two big photos were floating in it. He was looking at another one; he put the main light on as I went in and I saw it was the picture he'd printed in the school magazine.

'Fantastic!' he said. 'A lulu! Right round the twist. That's where they're going. You see what we've got here, Woolcott?'

'It's a picture of the Trust Deed,' I said.

'Bang on ! And you see what it's resting on?'

It was a really big photo. It was about two feet long. All the details in it were clearer than in the school magazine; he'd printed up much more of the photo, as well. At the top right-hand corner of it there was somebody's thumb, holding the document down. It was being held down on an open ledger. The detail was so clear you could even read what was in the ledger. It was a list of books, and the last line, half way down the page, said: *The Rose of Tibet – Lionel Davidson – Drifford*.

'It's on some kind of book,' I said.

'Exactly. The book ledger. That's where they list all the books they send from the county library to the little local libraries. And they'd just listed *The Rose of Tibet* as going to Drifford when I took the photo. We've got 'em cold. See why?'

'Not exactly.'

'Well, wake up, boy ! That item will be dated. Every book they send out is dated. So this photo is dated ! My God, it's almost *timed* ! The Chief Librarian could probably tell you to a quarter of an hour when that last line was written, and more lines were written after it. But they hadn't been then ! I photographed the thing as soon as we got it out of the parcel and into the light. Which means that, whether the Deed is authentic or not, at least this is a true copy of it. And here's further evidence to prove it.'

He picked another photo from the sink. It showed the document from a different angle, evidently taken from further back. It showed more of the arm of the chap holding it down, and a bit of his nose. It seemed to be the Chief Librarian.

'And this !'

The other picture in the sink was the second one he'd printed in the magazine. It showed the librarian grinning away as he held the document up. And he'd printed more of this picture, too, because you could see two other fellows also grinning away in the background.

'And they follow on the roll of film, one after the other. Couldn't be faked, you see. Taken within seconds of each other. Let them laugh that one off!'

I saw what he was so excited about now – and why he hadn't been able to keep his mind on Mike's problem.

It must have driven him mad, what they'd said in the paper about there being no legally-attested copy of the document. We'd been talking about it at school in the morning. Some people said the photo itself was a copy, and others that it wasn't, not a 'legally attested' one, anyway, because it could have been faked.

Moggy could have drawn the document himself and photographed it. You couldn't actually read the one the librarian was holding up. And even if all the experts came and said that what Moggy had photographed in his close-up shot was the document they'd actually seen, it still wouldn't make it a 'legally-attested' copy. It would only be an opinion, based on what they remembered.

For an 'attested copy', the geezer who does these things has to see both the original and the copy at the same time before he can give a certificate that it is a real copy. Either that, or there has to be some other guaranteed proof. And that's what Moggy's sequence of photos supplied.

As he'd said, they were taken within seconds of each other, one after the other. They couldn't possibly have been stunted up afterwards, not with the same bunch of people in them. And the middle photo, his close-up shot – and apparently it was the middle one of his three pictures – dated and timed it to show it had been taken immediately after the discovery.

'We're home and dry, home and dry,' Moggy said, and the buzzer rang. It was a different buzzer, from an intercom, and he went and answered it. 'Yes? O.K. Mrs Cripps, I'll take it,' he said, and switched off the intercom and picked up the phone. 'Morgan here!'

It seemed to be the local newspaper, and Moggy was very brisk with them.

'Certainly. Excellent pictures. I've done big blow-ups. Fill half the front page with them, if you want. The what? The film? Certainly not! That is the evidence, old boy – the order of the pictures on it. I'm hanging on to that. In fact, I'm doing better. I'm shoving it in the bank vaults this afternoon – and dammit, I'll have to run. They'll be closing in twenty minutes . . . Yes, Barclays Bank in George Square. Have ten photographers there, if you want. Jolly good. I'll bring my prints in to you afterwards . . . Woolcott!' he said, slamming down the phone.

'I'm here,' I said, because by his tone of voice he seemed to think I was in the next street.

'What kind of a hand are you with a glazer?'

'I don't know.' I'd never heard of one.

'Now's your chance to learn. I've got a couple of things to do. Get cracking over here.'

The glazer was an electric machine with a glossy heated plate that dried the photos and put a glaze on them, and he showed me how to do it, while he fiddled with something else. It was hot in the darkroom, and I saw why he was just wearing swimming trunks. There wasn't much room there for two of us. He kept muttering and swearing, and occasionally cackling out loud. He seemed to be winding something, and as we were back to back, I kept collecting a dig from his elbow. Then he finished and went out and started blundering around next door, and after a few minutes he yelled, 'Is your door open, Woolcott? I can't see.'

'Yeah, it is.'

'Well, shut it.'

'It's a bit hot in here.'

'Goddam it,' he said, and climbed down from somewhere and came and shut it himself. I heard him locking it, too.

I said, 'Here. What's that for?'

'For about half a minute,' he said.

And about half a minute it was. He was grinning when he opened the door again. He was coming out with little chuckles, too, and tapping his nose.

'Softly-softly, eh?' he said.

'Eh?'

'Exactly. Hic-hic-hic.' I'm trying to put what it sounded like. It sounded as if he'd gone off his head. I thought he had.

'Fishy things going on in this town, Woolcott,' he said.

'Is that right?' I said, carefully.

I read somewhere you don't want to argue with a madman. You don't want to annoy him.

'It's not right, but it's true,' he said. 'So to fix them up you've got to go in for a bit of fishy business yourself. Eh?'

'Yeah. Yeah, I suppose so,' I said.

'You couldn't be more right. Dead fishy! Hic-hic-hic,' Moggy said. 'Well, how are they doing now, those things?'

'I think they're doing all right, Mr Morgan,' I said carefully. 'I'm not quite sure how they're supposed to be doing.'

'Let's have a look. Mm. Still a bit tacky. Give 'em another couple of minutes. I think I'll go and put my trousers on,' Moggy said, and went out, and I looked after him, and wondered if I ought to beat it now, down the stairs and out of the house, as quietly and quickly as I could.

He didn't seem to have turned nasty, though. He was still chuckling away. I could hear him at it, as he hopped about pulling on his trousers in the bedroom. Before I could make my mind up, he was back again, looking quite normal. He had a jacket on, and a rolltop sweater underneath it, and he'd brushed his hair and smartened himself up.

'Well, now,' he said, and had a look at the prints and took

them off the glazer. 'First class. They'll do.' He waved them about a bit, and got a big stiff envelope and shoved them in. 'And most important of all – Exhibit Number One.' He opened a drawer and took out a roll of film. 'Cast your eyes on this, my boy. The next eyes to see it will belong to those lunatics on the committee.'

He'd taken a box from the drawer, and he put the film in and stuck it up with brown paper tape, and spent a minute or two fussing about looking for a pen to write his signature across the seal. Then he said, very briskly, 'Okidoke! . . . Where are you going now, Woolcott?'

'Nowhere. I mean, home,' I said, flustered. 'Union Street.'

'On the way to George Square?'

'Yeah.'

'O.K. I'll give you a lift. We're off.'

I wasn't too sure about this. He wasn't acting so weird now, but he was excited – and a crazy driver, at the best of times. I'd seen him. I followed him uneasily downstairs, and he yelled to Mrs Cripps where he was going, and she called back, 'Righto dear,' and we went out to the street.

He had his little M.G. parked farther along, and he gave me the envelope to hold as we got in, and started up, cursing a bit as he looked at his watch. It's one-way, Waterloo Street, with no turn-offs till Lancaster Lane, so he went up it like a rocket. He turned right into Lancaster Lane, tyres screaming, and then cursed a bit more. There are a few small driving schools in the side roads off there, and you usually get a few old jobs swaying about the road with L-plates.

There was one there now, and he hooted it, and after a bit of weaving managed to overtake it, and at the end of the road started swearing again. It's all clogged and narrow in that part of town, and at the end of the road there's usually a few post office vans parked, from the post office round the corner. One started pulling out as we got there, and Moggy sat fuming and gave the chap the benefit of his horn while the thing straddled the road. The driver took so long over it, Moggy looked back to see if he could reverse and get down one of the side streets. Only he couldn't, because the old job with L-plates had come up behind and was blocking him. And as I looked at it myself, I suddenly saw a weird thing happen. The front doors of the L-car opened and two men without faces got out.

It took a moment or two to see they had stocking masks on.

I don't think I was frightened. I think I was just curious. I didn't seem to connect it with us. But I looked to the front and saw the same thing happening with the mail van. The back doors had opened and two fellows with stocking masks had come out of that, too.

The four of them ran to our car, and without a word wrenched the doors open and just yanked us out. I could hardly believe it was happening. It seemed crazy, somehow, something I was watching on TV. But it was happening, all right. And just like when you fall, and don't feel anything for a second, but know it's going to hurt like heck in a minute, that started happening, too.

The bloke who'd yanked me out had picked me up by the back of my collar. I was half choked. And he just threw me out. He threw me out like a sack, and I landed in the street on my shoulder, and another bloke picked me up, and ran to the mail van and threw me inside.

I was so shocked, I didn't even struggle. I mean, it wouldn't have done any good if I had, but I didn't – I just mention it. And I landed in a huddle in the van, but facing out backwards so I could see through the open door what was happening to Moggy.

He wasn't putting up much of a struggle, either. He was just bent over, trying to protect his head, and a bloke with a piece of iron was trying to hit him on it. Another chap was forcing Moggy's hands away, and just as I watched, he managed it, and the one with the iron caught him a sickening clonk. I heard it. And he just folded up, and they picked him up before he fell, and staggered to the van with him, and bundled him in as well, and got in behind him, and before they closed the doors, I saw what the other two were doing. One was getting back in the L-car, and one had got in Moggy's, and we all started off together. I don't think it had taken two minutes, the whole thing.

I'd thought it was dark in the van, but it was only after the daylight. They had a light switched on there. In the light, I saw there was another geezer lying on the floor. It was a postman, and he was tied up and gagged, and watching us.

The men had gloves on, and they started searching Moggy. They found the box of film, but they went right through his pockets and took his wallet and his keys and all his papers, as well. I remembered I'd been holding the envelope of photos in the car. They must have got that as well now. Then I realized it didn't matter, because they'd got the film, anyway. I'm putting all this just as I remember it, but it wasn't as clear as this. In fact, I was so scrambled, it didn't even occur to me till they got the box of film and had a good look at it, why we'd been attacked at all.

The weird thing was, nobody said anything. They hadn't said anything when they'd first come swarming at us, and they never said a word now. They just got on with the job, and they didn't take long over it. The van had been driving along, and one of them moved over and gave a few bangs on the back wall, and after a while the thing slowed and stopped, and nobody moved for a bit, and then the doors were opened from the outside, and the two men got out. And the doors were locked again.

The postman was wriggling about and beckoning with his

head to me, so I untied and ungagged him, and he said, 'My goodness me!' He was a Welshman, and he kept saying it. 'My goodness me! Oh, my goodness me, what have they done to the poor man?'

Moggy was still spark out, and I was petrified he was dead, but his breath was coming. His head was bleeding. The postman kept rubbing his hands and saying, 'Oh, my goodness me,' so I thought I'd better do something. I didn't know what to do. I was frightened to touch Moggy in case something was broken, but I dabbed the blood with my handkerchief, and then saw there was a lot more under his head, and a handkerchief wasn't much good, so I took my shirt off and tried with that.

While I was doing it, the postman started hammering on the walls and yelling. But it took half an hour before someone got a policeman and we were out of there.

Moggy still hadn't come to, so I waited with him till the ambulance came.

8

I just read over what I put and I see I left a lot of things out.
There were too many things going on just then, so I better
go back and fill in.

I didn't even say anthing about the mural or the exhibition, or Nixon's bike or Soldier. I don't even know where to
start now. I suppose I better start with the bike, because it
looks as if it got forgotten – except not by me, it didn't, and
not by Nixon, either.

I was chatting over it with Mike and Soldier one time (it
was the time he forged the Cobbler's letter), and Soldier said,
'What's such a bargain he's offering you?'

I said, 'Well, it's not much of a price.'

'It's also not much of a bike.'

'Four quid's cheap for any bike.'

'Not any bike,' Soldier said.

He doesn't have much money, Soldier. He knows what
you're supposed to get for every bit of it. He's mechanical, too.
He knows about several things. He said, 'Let's see, it's a three-
speed Wellard, right?'

'Right.'

'M'hm. And it wasn't even new when he got it. I remember. How's the tyres?'

'O.K. I suppose.'

'And the saddle? And the brakes?'

He kept asking how this was and that was.

I said, 'Look, I don't know. It's a bike. It goes. The guy in
the bike shop offered him five quid for it anyway.'

'Who said?'

'He said.'

'The guy in the shop said?'

'Nixon said.'

'H'm. I'd ask the guy in the shop about that.'

'I can't do that. They know me there, anyway.'

'I'll do it,' he said. And he did.

I went with him. I didn't go in. I just hung about looking in the window of the shop next door, till I realized it was full of knickers, and a woman was looking back at me through the window, so I moved on and looked at soap-powder in the supermarket.

Soldier came out a few minutes later, grinning.

'Some bargain you got!' he said.

He'd gone in and said he wanted a second-hand, three-speed Wellard. The guy there said it was a funny thing, he'd got one coming in in a week or two from a customer who was buying a new bike. Soldier asked him what kind of condition it was in, and the chap said not bad but it needed a clean-up and the cable fixing on the three-speed, and it would cost five quid.

'Before it's fixed?' I said.

'After. Before, you can have it for four quid.'

'But that's what Nixon is giving it to me for.'

'Some bargain!'

'Well. Maybe the chap's offering Nixon more for it because he's buying the new bike from him.'

'Maybe,' Soldier said. 'And maybe not. All that concerns you is that when he offers you the bargain again, you'll know what to tell him.'

'He probably won't offer it again.'

'Oh yes, he will,' Soldier said. 'And if you want to know, I don't think the guy is giving him more than *three* quid for it. So Nixon can give it for that also. Don't pay a penny more.'

'You think so?'

'I know so. I'll do it, if you want.'

'No, I better do it.' Everybody knew Nixon and me were friends. 'If you're right,' I said.

'I'm right all right.'

Nixon had been keeping out the way of me lately. He *seemed* to have been. It's hard to say with him. He's a complicated geezer. He keeps a quarrel going a long time. He likes you running after him. I'd see him somewhere, say, and go towards him, and when I got there, he wouldn't be there. It happened too often to be an accident. Still, it might have been. I thought I'd stop running after him and see what happened.

A couple of days later he backed into me during break, and pretended to be surprised.

'Hi, then,' he said.

'Hi.'

'Haven't seen you much lately.'

'That so?'

'That bike's coming next week,' he said.

'Yeah?'

'I don't want the old one hanging about.'

'I suppose not.'

He was fiddling with a ball and looking as if he couldn't care less about the bike.

'You interested or not?' he said.

'Not.'

'Eh?'

'Not.'

'Not?' he said, stupefied.

'That's right.'

'Why?'

'Well, I want something a bit cleaned-up and with a decent gear. That kind of thing.'

'What's up with my gear?' he said. He'd gone a bit red.

'I never said anything was up with it.'

'Any old three-speed needs fixing.'

'Well, that's what I mean.'

'I mean, the price is a joke. But if it would help – I mean, if you want to get the gear a hundred per cent – I'd drop half a quid. To make it easier for you,' he said.

'Yeah?'

'How's that, then?'

'You see, there's still the drag of cleaning it up,' I said.

'Well, dammit, Jim,' he said. He hardly ever called me Jim. He was looking a bit panicky. 'I mean – don't you want it at all?' he said.

'I really wanted something in nice condition,' I said.

'How about if I dropped a whole quid?'

'What would that be, for the bike?'

'Three quid. I mean, it's ridiculous. It's only because we're friends.'

I still had an idea to tell him to get stuffed. At that price, the bloke in the bike shop could be his friend. But I remembered we were friends after all, and there was more to him than that, and he couldn't help being dodgy about money, and he did want me to have the bike. I had to leave him with some feeling he was doing me a favour. So I said, 'O.K. Thanks.' And he said with relief, 'That's all right. I'd like to do you a favour. Shake.' And we shook on it and grinned at each other, so that was O.K. again.

I got the bike, and he got the scare, and I cleaned it up myself, and the gear didn't bother me anyway; so it only cost me three quid.

Soldier fixed all that. It showed again he was reliable, dead reliable, and that Nixon wasn't. I had to remember that later.

It wasn't a thing Mike was ever likely to forget. He never did forget things about people. It was only his lessons he was dozy at. He never forgot what Soldier had done for him, with the Cobbler's letter. He started looking after him, after that.

A lot of the young kids used to twit Soldier about his accent and shove him around. (He's only small, Soldier.) They didn't after Mike showed up. He didn't thump them. He never thumped anyone. He didn't have to. He only had to show up, and the kids got lost.

He started including Soldier in the various things we were going to do during the holidays. We were going fishing for a couple of days, beyond Drifford; also to the fair. There's a fair every year at Easter. They put it up in the old railway parcels depot behind Waterloo Street. Mike said that since I had an extra quid, Soldier ought to get the benefit of some of it at the fair.

I remember we were going to do all that. We were going to do a lot of things at Easter. And we did, too; only they weren't the ones we planned.

That's what we were going to do; only I haven't said about end of term yet. We had to speed up with the mural the last week. We were breaking up Thursday, and the mayoress was unveiling the mural Tuesday; so to be on the safe side, Moggy wanted the whole thing up on the wall the weekend before.

We finished our bit in time. One of the other classes had a mess-up, but the whole thing got organized, and Pike, the twit who does woodwork, was put in charge of getting it all up on the wall. Some of his mates came in to help him, but they made such a big deal of climbing up and down ladders and flashing their carpenters' pencils and yelling, 'A bit more this end, Charlie,' that Moggy had to go and take charge of it himself, and Mike went with him. They worked all the weekend, and when we went in Monday, there it was, all round the walls, covered with sheets.

The mayoress came and did the job Wednesday, and

pulled various strings and the sheets fell off, and it looked great. In fact, it looked fantastic. It lit up the whole hall, and nobody had ever seen it looking as good before.

She made a speech saying how proud of us the town would be (they were opening up the school Easter week so people could go round and see it), and also how beautifully the mural was mounted. And Pike was so chuffed about what he thought he'd done that when our class had woodwork, right after, he let me take my tie-rack home. He was going round looking at all the gear made during the term and smiling away to himself, and he said, 'Well, boy, what's this, then, eh?'

'A tie-rack,' I said.

'Sir,' he said, a bit absent-mindedly, still smiling to himself.

'Sir. It's a tie-rack, sir.'

'A tie-rack, eh? A tie-rack. Not quite right, is it?' he said. The clumsy idiot had pulled the rack right out.

'No, not *quite* right, sir,' I said. 'Not now, it isn't.'

'Never mind. Nice bit of wood. Know what wood it is, eh?'

'It's mahogany, sir.'

'That's right. Mahogany. Come up nice if you plane it *that* way. That way, see.'

'I see, sir. Thank you very much for telling me, sir.'

'That's all right, lad. We've all got to learn, haven't we? Get a thing right and people are proud of you. Nice to have people proud of you, Woolcott.'

'Is it, sir?'

'It is. Very nice. Yes. Nice bit of wood. A lot of satisfaction in a nice bit of wood. All right, lad. You can take it this time.'

'Oh, thank you, sir.'

I took it. I took it out during break. I could hardly bear to look at it any more, but I had one last look while I said a couple of things to it. Then I threw the flipping thing as far as I could. It landed somewhere at the back of the science-block roof, and Pike was dead right. I got a lot of satisfaction out of it.

So all that was going on, and the exhibition got opened, too, the same Wednesday (though it wasn't quite finished yet, but they opened it, anyway), and there was a lot of busyness and excitement in the air. There'd have been that feeling, anyway, because we were breaking up next day, and the fair was starting Saturday and various geezers were making up groups to go to it. But it was different this time because of all the other goings-on, and also because the Inquiry was starting the following Tuesday, and Moggy was going there with his evidence, and some of us were going to give him a bit of a cheer as he went in.

But that was Wednesday, and the following day was Thursday, and in the early hours of it there was the break-in at the library and the evidence vanished; and just a few hours later Mike got the boot; and a few hours after that Moggy had his head bashed in; so there I was waiting with him till the ambulance showed up, and I think I filled everything in now.

9

I didn't go to the hospital with him. The police started questioning me even before the ambulance arrived, and when it did I had to go to the police station with them, and so did the postman. He didn't have much to tell. He said he'd been sitting in his van when, goodness me, a man with a stocking mask came and sat in it with him and showed him an iron bar and beckoned him to go in the back.

They hadn't hurt him. They just took his keys and tied and gagged him, and only minutes afterwards he saw me being thrown in the van, and that's all he knew. He couldn't describe the men because of the stocking masks, and he wouldn't recognize their voices because nobody said anything.

I didn't have any more to tell, really, but I had to keep telling it. While I was doing it, they got information that Moggy's car had been found together with the L-car. They'd both got parking tickets for being in a no-parking zone. This struck me as a bit of a giggle for Moggy and I looked forward to telling him it. But I wasn't able to do it for a bit. His skull had been split, and he didn't come to till Sunday.

It was all over the papers, of course, and the story got more fantastic still because the same night Moggy's flat got burgled.

(I don't want to give the idea these things go on all the time in our town. Hardly anything goes on. That's why all the TV people and reporters came down from London.)

Mike and I tried to get in to see Moggy Thursday, but couldn't, and so went again next day (it was Good Friday), and this time several policemen were there. It was supposed to be because of the reporters, but they were taking down the name of everyone who wanted to see Moggy, even ours; which seemed a bit queer.

I said, 'You know what, Mike? There's something fishy going on.'

'How d'you mean?'

'Something very fishy.' I suddenly remembered Moggy had used the same words, and I said, 'I'll tell you something else – I think Moggy had an idea this might happen.'

'What are you talking about?'

'I don't know. That's what bothers me.'

'Are you feeling all right?' Mike said.

I told him it all over again. I wasn't so much telling it to *him* as repeating it to myself, to try and remember every detail. I thought some magic thing would happen and I'd suddenly realize what Moggy had been yacketing about up in his flat. But nothing like that happened.

Moggy stayed unconscious meanwhile.

We tried again Saturday, and we tried Sunday. Nixon and Soldier had drifted along by that time, and a lot of other characters from school. The thing had got quite social. What with them taking your name every time, it was like calling at Buckingham Palace and leaving best regards for the Queen. Only this time it was different.

A policeman was standing behind the chap who took the names, and he leaned over when he saw mine.

'Woolcott?' he said.

'Yes.'

'Hold it.'

He had a word with someone on a telephone, and I heard him say, 'And who? ... Right.'

'Is there a Mitchell here?' he said.

'Yes. Here,' Mike said.

'This way.'

We looked at each other and followed him to a lift, and went up a few floors and walked along a corridor to a private room. A policeman was sitting outside it.

'Just one thing,' he said, before we went in. 'He doesn't know anything about his flat being burgled. The doctor doesn't want him told about it, all right?'

'All right,' I said.

Moggy was sitting up in bed drinking a glass of lemon. He looked as if he had a turban on. His smile was a bit crooked.

'How you feeling, Mr Morgan?' I said.

'Nothing like a relaxing sleep. They tell me I've been doing nothing else for three days.'

He wanted to know about the exhibition and this and that from Mike, but he had his eyes on me. They were a bit blood-shot, his eyes. He didn't look particularly scrambled, though; just thoughtful. He didn't say anything special to me. I had an idea he was trying to remember a couple of things, and not quite succeeding. It was only his words that were cheerful. His face wasn't. So I didn't tell him about the parking ticket.

It wasn't till we got out that I remembered it was me he'd asked for originally, not Mike.

There was a call for me the following day. My mum took it and she came back from the phone and said, 'It's the hospital, for you.' She looked a bit put out. They hadn't told her what it was about. Also we were in the middle of lunch. It was Easter Monday and she'd spent a lot of money on fresh salmon.

I went to the phone and someone asked me to wait, and a moment later Moggy was there. He said, 'Woolcott?'

'Yes, Mr Morgan?'

'What time is it?'

I had a quick glance at my watch and said, 'Quarter past one.' It's no use being surprised whatever he says.

'Quarter past one, eh?' he said. 'H'm.'

'How are you feeling, Mr Morgan?'

'It's Monday, of course, isn't it?'

'Monday, yes. Easter Monday, Mr Morgan. It's raining,' I said. You find yourself saying these barmy things to him.

'So I see. All the same . . . Do you think you could come and see me a little later – unless you're doing something?'

'Of course. Certainly,' I said. I'd been going to the fair with Mike and Nixon and Soldier. 'What time would be best?'

'I think – three would be *reasonable*, h'm?'

'Sure. Fine. Three.' I was going to say 'very reasonable', but stopped myself in time. It's very easy just to go on gibbering with him. 'Would you like Mike, too?' I said.

'Mike.'

'Mitchell.'

'Mitchell.'

'Would you?' I said.

'No.'

'Oh. O.K.'

'But bring him. H'm. Goodbye.'

'Goodbye,' I said, and looked at the phone for a bit.

I couldn't eat any salmon when I got in.

Mike and I went round, and gave in our names, and the policeman said, 'Woolcott. Yes. You can go up.'

'And Mitchell?' Mike said.

'No. Only Woolcott.'

'Oh,' Mike said. 'It's all right, it doesn't matter,' he said to me. He looked disappointed.

I went up and found the policeman outside the room again, and he gave me a nod and I went in.

'Hello, Mr Morgan.'

'Still raining, eh?' Moggy said. I had my raincoat on.

'It is a bit.'

He pulled himself up in the bed. He said, 'Woolcott, they won't let me out of here.'

'No.'

'And my flat has been burgled.'

I'd already figured he must know that. He had the newspapers all round him. 'I was sorry to hear it, Mr Morgan.'

'They can't tell me what was taken.'

'I thought nothing was taken. Mrs Cripps said so in the newspaper.'

'Yes, she wouldn't know. You and I are the only ones that would know, you see.'

I didn't say anything. He was stroking his turban. 'It's hard to remember,' he said frowning. 'I'm not totally clear on all that. You wouldn't remember, would you, if I had a little green book with me when we left the flat?'

I thought for a minute. I couldn't remember any green book. 'You had the photos in an envelope,' I said. 'And the film in your pocket. I don't remember a green book. Was it a big book?'

'No, a little green thing,' he said irritably. 'Like a pocket diary. You didn't see if they took it when they went through my pockets?'

I thought again. I still couldn't remember it. I remembered his wallet and his keys. There *had* been a pile of papers. They'd just snitched everything, very quickly. If he'd had it with him, they'd have got it. I told him all this.

He said gloomily, 'Well. I'll have to assume they've got it. It's the only thing that makes sense of the burglary. It's my exposure book, you see.'

'I see.'

'What do you see?'

I got confused. I hadn't seen anything. You just get in the habit of agreeing with him.

'It was your exposure book,' I said.

'Exactly. I write every detail in it. Half the film was blank, anyway. But I described every frame that was on it, together with the exposure, as an accurate guide for developing and printing.'

I just kept quiet about this. It seemed safest.

Moggy was looking slightly through me while he stroked his turban. 'I remember doing that, anyway,' he said. 'Because I copied the film just before you came. I had the prints washing in the sink. Then I copied the film, and wrote up the details in my exposure book. Then I heard Mrs Cripps's buzzer going, so I knew you had arrived, and I went and let you in. That right?'

' I don't know. I suppose so. You let me in, anyway,' I said.

'Exactly. And you started telling me something about Mitchell – that he'd been *dismissed*?'

'That's right.'

'How is he?'

'He's here. Downstairs.'

'I'm really sorry about that. I really am.'

'What was this film, Mr Morgan? What was it a copy of?'

'Of the other one.'

'What other one?'

'The evidence! Dammit, Woolcott, buck up! I just said so, didn't I?'

He hadn't said so, but he told me then. He said that before I got to his flat he'd been speaking to the newspaper on the phone, and they'd asked him for his film so they could make other prints. He said he'd make the prints himself. Then it occurred to him that the film was the only evidence he'd got, and that it would be a wise idea to copy it. As soon as he'd thought of this, he'd been nervous of having it in the house at all, and had thought of putting it in the bank. But he remembered feeling a bit edgy at even carrying it to the bank.

'I drove rather fast, didn't I?'

'Yeah. You did,' I said. 'But what about the other film? The copy that you made.'

'Well, that's it. I don't think I left it in the copying machine. I'm almost certain I rewound it. Can *you* remember?'

'Well, I wouldn't know, would I?'

'You would know. If I'd done it. I certainly hadn't rewound it before you came. I'd just copied it. If I rewound it at all, I must have done it while you were there. Try and think.'

I thought. I didn't even know what to think about.

'It was in a copying *machine*?' I said.

'Exactly. In the darkroom. Did you go in the darkroom?'

'Yeah, I did some glazing there. You asked me to.'

'Well, the copier's opposite the glazer. If I did it while you were there, we'd have had to stand back to back while I rewound.'

Just at that moment I did remember. I remembered getting his elbow in my back, several times.

'You did!' I said. It was weird to think of it, to realize suddenly what he'd been up to in there, when he'd forgotten it himself.

'I did?'

'Yeah!' I was doing a winding motion with my elbow.

'Exactly. Then what did I do with it?'

'I don't know.'

'Did I take it somewhere?'

'Wait a minute.' I tried to think. 'You went out of the room, anyway.'

'Where to?'

'To the next room.'

'The studio?'

'I *think* so. I can't be certain.'

'Then what?'

'I don't know . . . Wait a minute, you asked me to close the door.'

'And did you?'

'No, you did. You got down and locked it.'

'Why?'

'I don't know. I suppose –'

'I suppose I was hiding the film.'

'Yeah.'

'Where?'

'Look, Mr Morgan, I wasn't there,' I said. 'I was the other side of the door that you'd just locked.'

'I got *down* from somewhere, you said?'

I thought about this. 'If I said it, I suppose you did. I don't know what made me think that.'

Moggy thought about it, too. It didn't seem to get him anywhere. 'What happened after that?' he said.

'You opened the door again.'

'Did I say anything?'

'Well, you were – you were laughing.'

'*Laughing?*'

'Yeah.'

'I don't know what I had to laugh about,' he said, feeling his head. 'What kind of laughter?'

'Well. You were going hic-hic-hic.'

'Going what?' Moggy said, astonished.

'Hic-hic-hic – is what it sounded like,' I said apologetically.

'It did, eh? Well, do it again.'

'Hic-hic-hic,' I said, feeling a fool. He was staring at me.

'I wonder why I was doing that,' Moggy said.

'I don't know.'

'I just kept on with these animal noises? Or did I offer some other comment?'

'I think you said some fishy business was going on.'

'Still with the animal world, eh? Odd,' Moggy said. 'Hic-hic-hic,' he added, thoughtfully.

He didn't say anything for a bit. He just stroked his turban and looked at me.

'Well, that's the problem,' he said at last. 'I copied the film. I evidently hid it. I took my exposure book out with me. They must have found it. They realized there was another film in existence. And they burgled my flat to find it. The point is, did they find it?'

'Well. What would it look like?'

'It's a little cassette of film, thirty-five millimetre, about a couple of inches. I'd have wrapped it in silver paper.'

'Like a bar of chocolate?'

'More like a – little silver sausage.'

'Would you have put it in a drawer?'

'You say I climbed up somewhere.'

'It was just an idea. I don't know why I said it.'

'I'd stick with that. It's the kind of half-thing one remembers ... you say Mitchell is here?'

'Downstairs.'

'H'm ... I didn't want to involve others. I've got no right to involve you, only ... Dammit, I wish I could get out of here. It's Monday, isn't it?'

'Monday, yes,' I was going to say, 'Easter Monday. It's still raining,' but stopped myself in time.

'Tomorrow will be Tuesday.'

I started nodding to let him know he was quite right there, too, but suddenly saw what he meant. The Inquiry was starting Tuesday. That's what he was panicking about. At the same moment he said to me quietly, 'Is anyone outside there – in the corridor?'

84

'There's a policeman sitting there.'

'Well, come a bit nearer.'

I got a bit nearer. He lifted himself up further and leaned towards me, wincing as he held his head.

He said quietly, 'Listen, I've got no right to ask this, and if you want to forget it, do. But how would you feel about going back to see if you can find the film?'

I said, 'Well. Sure. But I don't know –'

'Exactly. And I can't help you. And not only that. If they found the film, that's the end of it. If they didn't, they might have someone watching the place.'

'Oh.'

'How do you feel about *that*?'

'Well.' I tried to think how I was supposed to feel about it. I didn't feel too good. I suddenly remembered the look of the men swarming towards us in their stocking masks; and how one of them had pulled Moggy's hands away while the other hit him. 'I don't know,' I said.

'It's not the physical danger, as such.'

'I see,' I said.

'You'd naturally have a look to see if anyone was watching. But you might feel nervous about going in there.'

'Yeah. I might,' I said. 'How about if I went in with the police?'

'No, no. I don't want that. The film's undeveloped. It can be destroyed in a moment by careless handling. The exposure was delicate, anyway. And enough funny business has gone on already. That document *should* have been copied, and it wasn't. And nobody was supposed to know where the thing was in the library, apart from a few council members. And somebody obviously did. Also, how did those chaps know I was going out just then? There's been too many funny mess-ups, and I can't risk another. It's not that I don't trust the police. I can't trust anyone. Except you . . . And Mitchell.

H'm. He has extraordinary intuition, an amazing visual gift...'

It was nice to have Moggy trust me, and to know Mike had his great visual gift; only I still didn't fancy getting my head bashed in because of it. I said, 'You see, Mr Morgan, I'm not really a hero or anything. I've never even been in the Scouts...'

He said, 'Oh, gosh, don't feel badly about it. Just forget it –'

'No, I don't want to forget it, Mr Morgan. I want to help. But – what would you do?'

'Well. I'd ring up Mrs Cripps and tell her to expect you. I mean, I'll do that, anyway. Then I'd shuffle over there and have a look round, and if the coast's clear, pop in. On your own up there you might be able to reconstruct – at least try and figure out where the devil I could have put it?'

'Are there many places you could have put it?'

'In the studio? – hundreds. It's only a tiny thing. Still, they apparently gave the studio a good going-over,' he said moodily.

They had. They'd tipped out all his brushes and tubes, and emptied his drawers, and taken things to pieces. The pictures stacked on the floor had been thrown everywhere, and those on the walls shifted to see what was behind them. It was quite a professional job, and they'd done it quietly. They'd got in with Moggy's own keys, and Mrs Cripps didn't even know about it till hours afterwards. She'd cleaned up what she could, and hadn't been able to find anything missing. She didn't know about this, though.

I said, 'Well, I'd like to think about it, Mr Morgan.'

'Do that. Consult Mitchell, if you want. And don't feel too badly about not doing it at all. Only if you want to do it, now would be a good time,' he said, looking out of the window. 'It's why I asked you to call now. Won't be dark for an hour or two. I shouldn't put the light on up there.'

'Oh. No.'

'Not that I think there's any danger.'

'I see. O.K., then. I'll phone you.'

'And let's have a bit of phone security now. Don't mention anything directly. Also, in case anybody happens to be listening, don't use your own name. You can call yourself . . . Bob.'

'Bob.'

'Mm. Nice name, Bob. Brave.'

'Right. I hope you feel better, Mr Morgan,' I said, and went out, a bit thoughtfully. I didn't feel too much like brave Bob yet.

Nixon and Soldier were waiting with Mike when I got down. They'd apparently rung up about the fair, and my mother had told them I was at the hospital.

'How is he?' Mike said.

'Fine. Fine. Look, I just want to have a chat with Mike,' I said to the other two. 'Moggy had a few things he wants me to tell him.'

'Why didn't he tell him himself?' Nixon said.

'He can't have too many visitors.'

'That's O.K.,' Soldier said.

'How about the fair, then?' Nixon said.

'You go on. We'll join you.'

'How long these discussions going to take?'

'I don't know. We'll meet there.'

'Ah, we'll wait,' Nixon said.

He wasn't all that keen on getting early to the fair. He was just jealous. I knew him.

'We can start walking, anyway,' I said.

So they walked on, and we followed, and I told Mike.

He listened without a word, just nodding, but when I'd finished he couldn't seem to understand what I was anxious about.

'What is there to it?' he said.

'Dammit, Mike. Moggy's up there with his head in bandages for just the same thing.'

'He wouldn't put you in danger. He said so.'

'Yeah, well. I don't know if he's quite normal now. He's still got concussion, you know. He *hasn't* got any right to ask it. I don't think he would if he was quite right in the head. He knows the house might be watched.'

'If it's being watched, you won't go in. What are you on about?' Mike said. 'Look, if you want we'll do it together. We won't only look in the front. We'll look at the back as well. We'll look all round everywhere. We won't take risks. We daren't take them, not if the film's still there.'

'What if somebody turns up while we're *in* there?'

'We'll look out the window. Or I'll go down. We could do that, anyway. I'll go down and see if the coast is clear, and if it is, I'll signal.'

'And if it isn't?'

'You'll stay where you are.'

'And what about you?'

'What about me?'

'You might have the film.'

'But I won't. Oh,' he said.

'Yeah. How do they know that?'

His face creased up, and then it uncreased. He said, 'You'll phone the police. There's a phone up there.'

'And what's happening to you meanwhile?'

'I'm running. Or something. Look, we have to do it for Moggy. He's lying up there.'

'Yeah. And we can end up lying there with him.'

'Jim, there isn't any risk. Well, there's just this tiny risk of someone turning up while we're there. But that only concerns me, doesn't it? And I'm prepared to take it. And I wouldn't if I thought there was any real danger.'

I looked at him. He'd gone back to Lepic's that night when

there'd been danger, and he hadn't been able to see it. Or if he had, he hadn't taken any notice of it. Still, it was true there wasn't much here. The way he'd worked it out, it was hard to see any. If anyone was waiting in the street, he'd see them from the doorway. He wouldn't even have to go out. He'd only be going out there to signal me that everything was O.K.

'All right,' I said, and yelled to the others, and they slowed and waited for us.

I said, 'Look, there a complication with one of Moggy's things. It's about something he had in the exhibition,' I added truthfully.

'What?' Nixon said, truculently.

'Just something he's got on his mind. We have to go and fix it.'

'You want help?' Soldier said.

'No, there's nothing to it. You carry on.'

Nixon walked off right away. 'Come on, Soldier,' he called.

'You're sure there's nothing we can do?' Soldier said, going reluctantly after him.

'No. See you there.'

'Maybe!' Nixon said, turning round.

I could see he was in a flaming temper. He knew he was being left out of something. I just shrugged. I'd have to sort him out later.

We let them put a bit of distance between us, and then followed. Waterloo Street was in the same direction. We got to number 74 about four o'clock.

10

We went up and down past the house a couple of times, and then Mike sauntered casually up an alley to have a look at the back. He wasn't long. 'O.K.,' he said, and we went and rang the bell.

Moggy had phoned Mrs Cripps, but she still didn't open up till she heard our voices. She had the door bolted and chained and she was looking nervous.

'A man was going to come and put a new lock on,' she said. 'I suppose he didn't because of the holiday. You know the burglars have Mr Morgan's keys.'

'You don't have to be frightened, Mrs Cripps,' Mike said. He knew her quite well. 'I'm sure they won't come back.'

'I don't know, dear. I can't help worrying, anyway. The other lodger's away, you see, and I'm here by myself. I hardly like going out. But I've got to. I dread coming in again.'

'Mr Morgan didn't have a back door key, did he?' I said.
'No.'

'Well, the burglars won't have, either. You can go out that way. Then you can keep the front door bolted and chained.'

'Yes,' she said, uncertainly, 'It would mean coming in the back way in the dark. I won't be back till late.'

'Well, would you like us to come back and see you in?'

'No, no, dear. Thank you very much. I'm just being silly. It is a good idea. I'll do it. How long are you going to be here now?'

'I don't know. Till it gets –' I was going to say 'till it gets dark', because I remembered Moggy had said not to put the

90

light on. But I didn't want to frighten her, so I said, 'About an hour, I suppose.'

'Oh. Well. I'll be gone by then. I'll give you a call when I'm going. You'll be sure to go out the back way yourselves, then?'

'Sure. It locks by itself, does it?'

'Oh, yes. Here we are. The key to Mr Morgan's flat. Leave it under the mat in the hall when you go out, love.'

'O.K.,' I said, and we went up.

Mrs Cripps had evidently done a good job of cleaning up, and I couldn't see anything different with Moggy's flat, except it looked a bit tidier. His pictures were in the same mess, though, and stacked as I'd last seen them, and so was his painting gear and the pile of junk on the table.

We just stood for a bit and had a look round.

'Well, we know they've been through all this, anyway,' I said.

'I suppose he did take it out of the copier?' Mike said.

We went and had a look. It was dark in there, so I closed the door before putting the light on.

Mike seemed to know the copier, and he handled it carefully, trying the winder first. Then he opened it and had a good look inside.

'Nothing.'

We stood and looked at each other. It was hot and airless in there. I suddenly remembered it had been like that before. I tried to remember every detail of what had happened, and I said it out loud to Mike.

'I was standing here, this way, facing the glazer, and he called out to me to shut the door, and I said it was hot, and he said "Goddam it," and got down and shut it himself, and then he locked it.'

'You just said it again,' Mike said. 'You said he "got down". Where from?'

'I don't know. I been thinking about it. I haven't a clue.' I tried again to recapture the sound, but I still couldn't; just the impression of his footstep, a bit heavier. 'Maybe he just shifted his weight from one foot to the other.'

'But you said he had no shoes on.'

'He didn't. He was barefoot. No, he must have got down. Only I don't know where from.'

We turned the light off and opened the door and looked at the room again. There was no ladder. There was the table, the chairs. He couldn't have stepped down from the table; he'd have had to jump. It must have been a chair.

'Mm,' Mike said. 'What did he *say* – when he opened the door again?'

'He was laughing. I told you. He said fishy things were going on, and if you wanted to fix them you had to go in for fishy business yourself. He was tapping his nose when he said it,' I said, suddenly remembering.

'Fishy business,' Mike said.

'He meant funny business.'

'Yeah, but he said fishy. And he said it twice. Fishy things, and fishy business ... Tapping his nose,' he said thoughtfully.

'It was just like his hic-hic-hic. He was larking about and laughing. He could have waggled his ears.'

'Yeah, but he didn't. It was his nose. It was some connection with ... Fishy. It's to do with fish,' Mike said. He said it quite suddenly, as if he was certain of it. 'What was he doing with fish?'

'Unless he was painting one, he wasn't doing anything ... Not when I was there, anyway. He was doing the photos.'

'Fish,' Mike said. 'Could he have put it *inside* a fish, in his fridge?'

We had a look round. Moggy didn't have a fridge. While we were doing it, Mrs Cripps called from below that she was going.

Mike went out on the landing.

He said, 'Mrs Cripps – did Mr Morgan have any fish up here?'

'Fish? No, dear. He doesn't like fish. Do you want some? I've got a lovely bit of haddock.'

'Where is it?'

'Down here in the pantry. It's fried. I got it Saturday.'

'Oh,' Mike said. Moggy'd had his head bashed Thursday. 'No, thanks,' he said.

'It'll only go to waste. It's *beautiful* fish. Everybody's away, you see. I'll put a piece out for you.'

'No. No, don't bother,' Mike said. 'I was only wondering . . .'

'Oh, well. You'll remember to put the key under the mat,' she said, and we heard her muttering about an umbrella, and fiddling with it, and then she went. She went out the back way.

Mike came back in the room and stood on a chair, and I thought for a moment he was trying to see if it was possible to catch a fish in the air. He was stretching both arms out.

'What was it he could only reach from a chair?' he said.

'The picture rail?'

Mike had a squint along the picture rail, and I got a chair and had a squint along another. There was nothing there. The burglars had been this way, anyway. They'd even looked behind the pictures that were hanging from the rail.

'What are we looking for?' Mike said.

'The film. Idiot.'

'No, I mean, what's it look like?'

'It's about two inches long, wrapped in silver paper. He said it looks like – a little silver sausage,' I said, remembering.

'Or a little silver fish,' Mike said.

'Look, forget fish,' I said. He seemed to have got one-track about it. 'It was just a joke.'

'H'm. Well. Would he have taped it to something?'

'Maybe. Wait a minute. He had the tape in the dark-room. He came in and got it to tape up the other film. He got it out of a drawer in there. But that was afterwards. He'd already hidden this one.'

'He might have had more tape out here.'

'Yeah, he might.'

'What would he have reached *up* to tape it to?'

'The skylight?' I said.

Mike shifted his chair under the skylight and got up again and tried to reach it. He's bigger than Moggy but he still couldn't.

'Maybe with a pole?' I said, and went around and tried to find one. The only thing I could find was a mop in the bathroom. Mike tried with that, and reached the skylight easily, but he couldn't open it.

'It hasn't been opened for years,' he said, poking away.

'Well, leave it. I don't see how he would have got it up there, anyway, on the end of a pole.'

I'd had another idea. I'd got it in the bathroom, but it only just hit me then. There was an old-fashioned toilet in there, the kind where you have to pull a long chain. The cistern was up on the wall. If you wanted to hide something there, you'd have to step *up* on the toilet seat . . . and step *down* again.

I went back and had another look, and was suddenly sure of it. The bathroom was just off the studio. *That's* what Moggy had been laughing at – hiding a valuable film in the toilet. I stood on the seat but couldn't reach the cistern. Moggy could have reached it. Mike could reach it.

I said a bit faintly, 'Mike, could you come here a minute?'

'Hang on,' he said.

I hung on there, excited and trembling.

'Mike, come on.'

He said, 'Jim, I found it.'

'Eh?'

'I found the film, Jim.'

I got down and went in the studio. Mike was standing on the chair, looking a bit sick. He had the silver-paper-wrapped film in his hand.

'Where was it?'

'In the fish.'

'*Where?*'

'There.'

He was pointing to Moggy's barmy picture with a tin can stuck on it. It was a sardine can. The film had been in the sardine can. The can had been opened with a key, and the key was still in it, with the top wound back, forming a roll. Moggy had unwound the roll a bit and stuck the film in it. It wasn't out of sight, or anything. You just didn't notice it. The silver paper was the same colour as the tin; the whole lot had become part of the picture.

Mike was staring at me with his mouth open, as if I'd found it.

I suddenly realized my own mouth was open, too.

I said, 'O.K., Mike. Come on,' and he got down, and we both still stood looking at each other. It was so weird, we hardly knew what to do. He gave me the film and I put it in my pocket, and went and looked out of the window. It was raining out there, and already getting dark. It was pretty dark in the room, too. The rain was drumming on the sky-light. It must have been going on some time, and we hadn't noticed. It was obvious there was no one in the street, but I thought we better keep to the plan, all the same.

'Remember, don't put the light on as you go down,' I said.

'O.K.'

I put the mop back in the bathroom and straightened the chairs while he went downstairs, and I heard the front door slam behind him, and at the same moment remembered he wasn't supposed to go out that way, anyway. It didn't matter, so long as I remembered to bolt and chain it myself and go out the back way, but it showed how you could forget things out of excitement. I decided that was the last mistake we were going to make till the film was safely at home, and I could ring Moggy; and I went over to the window, and saw Mike skipping across the road in the rain.

I couldn't see him properly through the streaming window, but he started signalling. Only as well as forgetting about the front door, the clot had forgotten the signal, too. He was supposed to hold his right arm up and wave it. He was waving both arms at me. I realized he couldn't see my return signal through the window, so I tried to open it, and found it jammed and had to strain and push at it. By the time I got it open, he'd gone.

That was funny.

I hadn't signalled back.

Or had he thought I *had*, when I was pushing at the window?

He must have done. He wouldn't have gone, just to get out of the rain, without seeing my answering signal. That's what came of being excited; so I carefully closed the window again, keeping my own excitement down, and let myself out of the flat and locked Moggy's door behind me; and in the same moment heard the front door shut again below.

That was *very* funny.

I had three quick thoughts about it. The first was that Mike had come back in again. The second was that he couldn't have done, because I'd heard the door slam behind him and he didn't have the key. The third was that it must be Mrs Cripps; except she'd said she wouldn't be coming back till late.

While I was thinking all this, I was letting myself back

into Moggy's flat again, and locking the door, and standing with my ear to it, listening.

Someone was coming upstairs. Quietly. Heavily. It was a man.

I thought. *Oh, Gawd!* and tried to think what we'd planned if things went wrong. I was supposed to put the film back wherever it was hidden, and ring the police.

It was getting very dark in the room now. I could just see the phone. I got over to it, and lifted the receiver, and in the same moment heard a little tinkle below, and nearly fell through the floor. The phone bell was evidently downstairs, and it tinkled if you picked up the extension phone. Whoever heard that knew someone was trying to use the phone upstairs. I'd left the key in my side of the door, though. The man coming upstairs wouldn't be able to get in, even if he had a key. And if he heard me calling the police, it might throw a scare in him, anyway.

My heart was pumping away, and I could hardly think. I found 9 on the dial, and dialled 999; only while I was still dialling a man's voice said in the receiver, 'Put the phone down, son. You can't call anyone while this one's off, and it's staying off. Just open the door up there, and you won't get hurt.'

My heart practically stopped. I felt myself freeze up. Two of them, then. One coming up the stairs; one below. I put the phone down, very quietly – as if there was any point in doing it quietly – and stood for a petrified moment looking round the room. It had got very dark. I took the film out of my pocket and was actually pulling the chair into place to climb up and put it back in the sardine can, when I thought: No. *I'm not doing it. I'm not going to open the door. I'm not going to tell them anything. I'm not going to leave the film, either. I'm getting out with it. Only how?*

I shifted over to the back window. Moggy's table was

jammed up against it, piled with his junk. I couldn't reach the window properly, so I got on the table, and crouched there, and opened the catch, and pushed, and found this window was jammed, too.

I'd more or less stopped breathing. I was in such a panic, I'd practically stopped thinking, too. I shuffled forward on the table, and got my shoulder near the frame, and gave it a good nudge, and nothing happened, so I got back about a foot and just barged at it. I heard the key going in the door lock while I did this, and the chap rattling the handle, and in the same moment the window burst open, and I nearly flew out of it.

My feet slithered out from under me, and bits of Moggy's junk went skidding behind me on to the floor. I'd clutched at the window, and I hung on to it now for dear life, and felt rain pelting at me, and realized half of me was outside, and the ground was three floors below.

I frantically scrabbled with my feet and got them back in position and slowly drew myself in, and poised there a moment, looking about me. There was no drain-pipe handy. The nearest drain-pipe was on the far side of the house, to the left. The house was the end of a terrace, and the alley was there. I had a look to the right, and saw it would have to be that. The place next door was called Temperance Hotel. They'd turned it into flatlets, and added another floor, and the council had made them put a fire-escape up, and thank God they had.

The fire-escape was there, an iron spiral, glistening with rain, but about eight feet away. There was nothing in between. There was just the window-sill of this room, and then a slab of wet brick wall, and the fire-escape : eight feet away. I had a look upwards, and saw a rain-water gutter above me. Water was pouring off the sloping roof. I could hear it guzzling along the gutter. If I could get on the window-sill, and hang on to the gutter, I could – what? Reach over with one of my eight-foot arms and grab the fire-escape? It needed a rope, or a hook, or a . . .

Or an anchor.

The moment I thought of it, I was already back inside the room and searching the table. The anchor wasn't on the table. It must have been one of the things that went flying. I got down on the floor, and heard the door rattling, and the chap said, 'If you don't open up, I'll break in. And you'll know about it!'

I said, 'Hang on. The key's stuck. Is your key still in?'

'Yes.'

'Well, take it out, and I'll try again.'

I searched about on the floor while he did it, giving the door the occasional kick to keep him happy, and he said, 'O.K., it's out,' I said, 'Right. I'm trying. The key's bent. Just a minute, I'll try and lay hands on something,' and the same moment I laid hands on the anchor.

'What you doing in there?' he said.

I gave the door a kick and said, 'It's really bent. It's bent right over.' And so it was. The anchor was beautifully bent: I knew it would grip if only I could land it on the fire escape. 'I'm trying to get something through the handle,' I said. I seemed to be giving him a running commentary, because that's exactly what I was doing. The rope had come out of the anchor's handle. It just ended in a knot. I wasn't happy about that. I shoved the other end through and tied it with a double reef knot, and then made a running loop at the opposite end.

'Oy! What you doing?' the bloke said.

'I'm tightening it. Try poking something through your end,' I said.

I was poking myself through my end. I got the running loop of rope over my head and lowered it below my arms, and tightened it there. Then I gave the door a final kick and got back on the table.

The rain was blowing straight in. The whole table was wet. I shuffled forward to the window, and got one foot out on the slippery sill, and wondered what to do with the other. I was perched there like a frog, half in and half out. I couldn't get both feet on the sill.

I leaned forward on the open window frame and grimly tested as much of my weight as I could; and then went further and put all my weight on it, and hung there, and looked up.

The gutter was a couple of feet above the window opening. Not too far if I could push myself up on the window frame. It was creaking, though. It hadn't been opened for a long time. I didn't know if the hinge would hold. I just prayed it would, and started pressing down on it and pushing more of my body up through the opening.

I went up inch by inch, craning my neck round to keep my eye on the gutter; and when I thought I could manage it, released one hand and made a quick grab, and caught the gutter, and held myself tilted there a moment, leaning out into space, one hand on the window frame and one on the gutter.

I couldn't stay there for ever, but the next bit was so much worse I could hardly bear to think about it. I had all my weight on the window now. The hand on the gutter was only holding me in position. To get all of myself out on the sill I was going to have to take the hand off the window and make a grab with it for the gutter. If I grabbed wrong, I'd just be grabbing air, and grabbing it all the way to the ground, three floors below.

This was so horrible, I didn't bother to think about it. I just did it. I paused a moment and took a breath, and tightened my grip on the gutter with one hand and lunged upwards with the other, and caught it, and hung there, sweating. I thought I was going to be sick.

I was twisted round at a funny angle. My feet were facing outwards and I was facing inwards. I clutched on to the gutter and carefully shuffled my feet round, and waited there a moment, feeling the water racing over my hands in the gutter, and then got one wet hand down, and felt for the rope, and pulled the anchor out of the room.

The fire-escape was to my left now, and I looked towards it, and judged the distance, and swung the anchor, and heaved, and got it first go, and pulled the rope tight; and then had another idea, and bent to the window. I could hear the door shaking in the room. I didn't want him bashing it in before I'd started down the fire-escape. His mate below could cut me off before I reached the bottom.

I poked my head through the opening and called, 'Stop shaking the door, then. You're only jamming it. Give me half a minute, can't you? I'm doing everything possible.'

Then I did something that didn't seem too possible.

I got both hands on the rope, and with the weirdest feeling that it was happening to somebody else and not to me at all, I stepped off the sill into space.

II

I wasn't breathing much at the time, so I didn't get the air knocked out of me. I just felt I'd been cut in two. The running loop tightened with such a yank, I nearly had my arms pulled out of joint. I'd been clutching the rope, to take the shock, but my hands were wet, and so was the rope; and so was I, wet through. I'd been in such a panic on the window-sill, I'd hardly noticed the drenching rain.

I hit the iron spiral, and bounced off it, and swung, and heard the anchor squeaking and grinding above. It was only a little anchor. It wasn't going to put up with much of this. I tried to hook a leg through an iron railing as I hit again, but skidded off it, and tried to time it as I came back again, and this time got a hand off the rope, and grabbed, and made it, and was hooked there for a moment, hand and leg round a railing; and I got the other arm up and hung on the hand-rail, and tried to pull myself up and over.

It was slippery, everything slippery, rain still pouring, but I managed to slither over after a struggle, and lay gasping on the steps like a stranded fish; which wasn't a bad description. I was still hooked on the line. I had to get off the line. I had to get moving. I knew all this, and couldn't. I felt paralysed with relief at being alive. I felt paralysed, any-way, the whole upper part of my body stiff. I had to rest. I knew I couldn't. Not here. In a minute or two, at most, he'd break the door open. I had to move now.

I pulled the loop loose and got it over my head and dragged myself upright, still gasping, and released the anchor, too. Mustn't leave the anchor on the fire-escape. I knew that. I didn't want any attention paid to the fire-escape at all. It didn't look possible to reach it. He'd see the window open, and figure I'd got on the roof somehow, or had fallen out. Either way, it would give me more time.

I looped the rope round my neck and started down, fast as I could. The stairs were slippery as an ice-rink, and I skidded right away and bumped down five on my behind, and pulled myself up and grimly hung on to the railing after that, skittering down like a little old woman; and hadn't got more than half way when I heard a yell.

I looked up and saw a light on in the room, and two heads peering out. Two heads. Both of them up there, then. They saw me the moment I saw them, and vanished, and I imagined them pounding down the stairs in there, and put on an extra spurt, and skidded again, and half choked myself when the anchor caught in a railing.

I was in such a panic, I hadn't a clue where to go. I knew I mustn't try for Waterloo Street. They'd be there before me. They'd probably have a car there. I was at the back of the house. I'd better stay at the back. Stafford Place was at the back. It was a cul-de-sac, blocked both ends. There were alleys through, though. I tried to remember where the alleys went; couldn't; mind blown with shock and fright.

There was a bit of a glow in the sky; lights on everywhere now. I had to get to the lights; to shops and people. No good running home. They might follow me home. There'd be safety in shopping streets.

I suddenly remembered there wouldn't be safety there. No shops open today; Easter Monday. Some Easter Monday! I had to get somewhere, though, and fast; and as I got to the bottom of the fire-escape, I saw this was going to be the main problem. It didn't go anywhere.

There was just a big back yard there, like a prison yard. There were walls about eight feet high all round it. I scampered about, looking for the back door to Stafford Place, and found it, and found the padlock on it, firmly locked, and searched desperately round for some other exit. There was only one other exit, the side door out to the street. I wasn't taking that: had to stay away from the street. How to get over the flaming wall, then?

I was thinking all this with the anchor round my neck, and the idea went off like a bomb in my mind, and the instant it did, I had the anchor off my neck and was heaving it, but changed my mind at the last moment. Not safe to go out to Stafford Place now. I'd wasted time running about in the back yard. Not safe to go out to it from here, anyway. They knew I was here. I'd better go over the wall to the next house, and work my way along.

I pitched the anchor to the top of the wall, and it caught, and I tugged hard and took the strain, and walked up the wall, hand over hand on the rope, and got to the top and kept my head down and scrambled over.

I landed in somebody's garden; evidently in the compost heap, smelly but soft, and grabbed the anchor and got moving again.

I went over half a dozen walls the same way, before chancing a look out to Stafford Place. There was no need for the anchor here. I found a back door with just a little latch that opened easily, and peered out, and saw them right away.

If the situation hadn't been so hairy I'd have fallen down laughing. They were outside the back of the Temperance Hotel, and one was standing on the shoulders of the other. He was trying to get over the wall. He managed it after a few shots, but the other chap must have had a bad time, because he stepped back rubbing his shoulders and swearing. I kept my head in.

They started calling to each other after a while, but I

couldn't hear what was said. Then it stopped, and I looked out, and saw the guy in Stafford Place walking away. He was walking fast, almost trotting. I worked this one out. The guy in the back yard must have found the side entry to Waterloo Street. Maybe they'd figured I'd gone out that way.

I gave it a minute or two to let him get well round the corner, and meanwhile scouted the position. There was an alley directly opposite me. I could see a street at the other end with lights. A motor bike and sidecar passed in it as I watched. That was the place for me. And after that street another street, till I was among people and could take it easy. They'd be searching some time for me here.

I waited a bit longer to be on the safe side, and then walked cautiously out and crossed the road to the alley; and as soon as I did, knew I'd backed wrong. I heard footsteps running, and looked round, and the chap who'd vanished round the corner was coming after me. He was coming fast. He hadn't been sent to the front. He'd been standing just round the corner, watching the street.

I took off like a jet. I had a hundred yards start on him, but he was pounding after me like mad. My heart was in my throat and painfully bumping there. It was only a little alley, and I shot out of it into the street – an empty street, dead empty except for two or three cars tooling along, and I knew I musn't get caught there.

I turned right, panting – and suddenly knew where I was making for. The glow in the sky I'd noticed from the fire-escape wasn't just the town lighting. It was from the fair. That's where all the people would be. That's where I had to be. I could hear it now. And something else : I knew exactly where I was. I could get to the fair if I just kept along this street. It led to the back of the old parcels depot, which is where the fair was.

But I wasn't going to make it on speed. He'd made up a lot

of distance. He'd seen which way I'd turned, and was following. There were plenty of side streets running off the opposite side of the road, and I crossed over, with the idea of breaking into one, to try and lose him. The flaming anchor was a drag on me, and I was going to drop it, when I suddenly had a new idea, and I put on a spurt.

There were little run-down shops round here. I picked one, a tailor's shop, with a deep doorway, in a patch of shadow, and jumped in it, and waited there. He knew I'd turned off somewhere, but he couldn't tell quite where. I waited, in a panic, trying to control my breathing. If he guessed where I was, I'd had it. I remembered what they'd done to Moggy. He wouldn't mess about asking me to give up the film. A couple of heavy thumps in the doorway, and he'd be going through my clothing ...

But if I'd out-guessed him, *he'd* had it. I guessed he thought I'd turned into another alley, and that he was keeping an eye open for it. He'd slowed down, anyway : I could hear that. He'd be looking in the doorways, too, of course. It wasn't a matter of just hiding there and fooling him. He wouldn't be fooled. He'd see me, and I'd see him. I wanted him moving while he did it.

As it happened, the clot didn't see me right away. He just ran slowly past, his ugly mug screwed up and peering ahead, and only caught sight of me from the corner of his eye. I stepped out of the doorway, and again, if it wasn't so hairy I'd have fallen down laughing. He was so surprised he practically went cross-eyed. He slewed round fast on the pavement, and I let him have the anchor quite slowly. I just bowled it at him, and caught his right leg, and it pulled out the rope, and I let him have that, too, and he got his left leg snagged in it, and went full length.

He was in the most beautiful tangle and swearing his head off as I passed him. I passed him like a champion, and a long time later heard him pounding behind me again. He seemed to be limping.

I kept on to the fair. I had an urgent date with Soldier – if I could find him. The chap knew what I looked like now. I had to get rid of the film.

12

It was about five o'clock when I got there, and the rain had slackened a bit. It always rains Easter, for the fair – I couldn't remember when it hadn't – but it never put anyone off going there. The place was crowded already, lit up like daylight, and with the most fantastic row going on – the Roller-Coaster and the Big Dipper roaring, loud-speakers blasting everywhere, from roundabouts and side-shows.

I loved it normally, only it gave me a headache now. I was wet through and worried, and aching all over. Even my behind was aching. I just wished I was in bed, and fast asleep, and that none of the crazy things had happened; apart from everything else, I was hungry as well. I hadn't had any lunch.

I knew Soldier didn't have much money, so he wouldn't be hanging about the expensive things like the Dipper; but Nixon had, and he would, and they'd probably keep together. It wasn't a question of going where the crowds were thickest. The crowds were thick everywhere. They were tramping round in the mud eating candy floss and hamburgers.

What you got to watch out for at our fair is the factory girls. They go round in groups and try and round up some poor geezer and kiss him. Plenty of them were roaming about now, singing, and I saw a gang forming near me, and got ready to run. A guy once told me if you cross your eyes and put your tongue out they think you're mad and leave you alone. I saw they already had someone, but I edged round sideways, and crossed my eyes anyway, and then saw who it was, and uncrossed them.

They'd got Mike.

Mike?

The big idiot was stepping from one foot to the other with about fifteen girls round him. I don't know if I said he's good-looking, Mike. He's tall. He's six foot one. He has this long blond hair. Three or four of the twits were stroking it, and others were slobbering at his ears and his nose. He was just letting them, shuffling about and grinning in a wet sort of way. He seemed to be grinning at someone. Quite a few people were standing about laughing, but I saw who he was grinning at. It was a stocky geezer with a bald head and a flattened nose, like an old boxer, and he wasn't grinning back. He was trying to push through, but the girls wouldn't let him.

I yelled 'Mike!' and his eyes came round and saw me, and he moved right away. He moved away from me! He just ducked out of it and vanished, and the only way I could tell where he went was by a trail of girls clutching after him, squealing.

I went after him, and saw the bald-headed geezer on the same track, and put two and two together, and realized he was following Mike.

I kept him in sight, but it wasn't so easy to keep Mike in sight. He got clear of the girls and broke through a queue waiting for the helter-skelter, and nipped round the back of it, and then went in a tent where they had the Ugliest Woman in the World. He just skipped the box-office and went past the chap who takes the tickets, and the chap said, 'Oy!' and went in after him. But the bald-headed geezer steamed in then, and the chap turned and caught him instead, and while they were still arguing the toss, I saw Mike creep out the back and break into a run, and I ran after him.

He turned and saw me and waved me away, and I called, 'Mike, wait! It's O.K.,' and he stopped and squeezed himself into an opening at the back of two stalls and waited for me.

He muttered, 'Stay away from me. Two guys are following me.'

'*Two*?'

'I had to hit one.'

'You what?'

'I had to,' he said apologetically. 'He had knuckle-dusters. I didn't do it very hard. He's having a rest behind a Wimpy stall. He'll be back, though. The other one's still around.'

'Mike, I've got the film on me.'

'Oh, no! Look, you were supposed to leave it there. We agreed. They'd never have found it! I signalled you.'

'There's no time – Is Soldier here?'

'Yeah. He saw me. I been keeping away. I didn't want to get him –'

'I've got to slip him the film.'

'Jim, no! You'll put him in –'

'I've got to! I'*m* being followed. I'll slip him it and tell him to scram off home quick.'

He said, 'Oh, Jeez. Look, I'll take it.'

'You won't. Idiot. It's the *only* film. They're on to both of us. They don't know anything about him. Where is he?'

'He was rolling pennies. Over by the Big Wheel. I don't know if –'

'O.K. Try and keep me in sight – but keep your distance. We'll join up afterwards.'

'Listen, Jim –'

'So long.' I moved away from him. I had my hands in my pockets and could feel the film there. It seemed to me everyone in the world must know I was carrying the flaming thing. It was a weird feeling, knowing it was worth a few million quid. I made for the main lane where you could see everything. It took time to push through the crowds in the mud. I got there and looked around, and saw the Big Wheel and started towards it.

There were several lines of stalls all round it, things like throw-a-dart and hit-the-moving-ball and bingo stands. I went round all the roll-a-penny places. He wasn't in any of them. Then I had a look round the wheel, and saw him there.

He was standing watching it fill up. Nixon was having a go, and hadn't bought him a go. He'd just gone along to watch. It suddenly struck me as an idea, the wheel. There were carriages for two. Each was separate from the others.

I came up behind him and said, 'Soldier.'

He spun round. 'Hello. I was wondering where you were. I saw Mike. He didn't see me.'

'Get in.'

'Eh?'

'Have a go. Get in!'

'No, it costs too much. You must get a good view up there, though,' he said, looking wistfully up to the top. I could see Nixon on top. He could see me, too. He gave a wave. I didn't wave back.

I said, 'Go on. My treat. Get in.'

'You mean it?'

'Get in!' I hissed. There's no box-office at the wheel. You just get in a carriage as it stops at the bottom, and a guy takes the money, and it moves up one, and goes on that way till they're all full, and then starts. It was nearly full now. There were only two people in front of us. They waited till a couple got out of a carriage, and then got in themselves, and we took the next one. The guy took the money, and snapped the safety bar in place, and waved, and the thing took off.

I didn't say anything till it went round a few times. It was true you got a great view up there. I looked around and tried to see Mike, and the plug-ugly who was following Mike, and the plug-ugly who'd been after me. I couldn't see any of them, just lights and shifting crowds of people. I saw Nixon from time to time as we swung round. He kept waving and grinning. I suppose he was trying to show how friendly he was and that it just never occurred to him to buy Soldier a go. He must have known I'd bought him one. He couldn't help being mean about money, Nixon, so I waved back after a while, and Soldier waved, too, and everybody was happy, and Soldier kept saying, 'Oh, boy, this is something, isn't it?'

'Yeah, it's something.'

'Oh, boy, it's great.'

'Soldier, I want to talk to you.'

'It's just fantastic,' Soldier said.

'I want to tell you something even more fantastic,' I said.

'It's even better than I thought it would be.'

'Ah, shut up,' I said, and told him.

The thing was going faster now. It was going really fast, and we were hanging on the safety bar. I was hanging on it with one hand. I had the other in my pocket round the film. There was a lot of row going on, too, and it swelled every time the carriage plunged downwards to the ground. He had to bend his head towards me. He practically had his ear in my mouth, so I couldn't see his face. I didn't see it till I finished, and he looked at me. I thought he might be scared, but if he was he didn't show it. He just said, 'O.K.'

'You got it?'

'Yes. I have to get off the other side from you and go home right away. You'll phone me. Give me it, then.'

'O.K. Wait.'

The wheel was going too fast for me to get it out of my pocket. I thought of something else, too. I couldn't see people on the ground, but they could probably see us. The only safe place was right at the top, where we were out of sight for a second. The wheel had to go very slow before I could time that.

We did a few more fast spins without saying anything. Soldier didn't even say it was great any more. Then it started slowing, and I planned it, and as we swung up to the top I got the film out of my pocket, and held it on the seat, and he took it, and slid it into his own pocket; and we were both hanging on the safety bar again as the wheel did the downward journey.

It did a couple more turns, and then they started letting us off. To get off, you had to go through the same business as to get on. The carriages stopped one at a time, and people got off and new people got on, and paid up, and the wheel swung round one place more.

This took time, and while we were doing it, I saw the guy who'd been chasing me. He was looking at me, as we came down in the carriage, and he wasn't looking very friendly.

'Goodbye, Soldier,' I said, without looking at him, and got out and walked right towards the guy. The idea was to take his attention off Soldier in case he happened to suspect anything. When I was near him, I pretended to see him for the first time, and broke and ran, and it worked. He followed me right away, and so did someone else.

'Woolcott!' It was Nixon. 'Hang on! Look, I won a few things.'

He had a glass vase and Cellophane bag of chocolates in his hand. I didn't answer him. I just wriggled through the crowds, and tried Mike's trick, breaking through the queue at the helter-skelter. Nixon was nippier on his pins than the plug-ugly, and he caught me the other side.

I hissed, 'Stay away!'

'What's up?'

I couldn't start explaining to him. I didn't want him to know anything about it, anyway. I thought I better just say something that would make him go away. He hadn't stopped running with me, so I said, 'Yeah, you hang on to your prizes *and* your money, you mean devil!'

'What?'

'Keep away from me. Beat it!'

He didn't say another word. He just stopped and I didn't see him again. I didn't feel good about it, but I had other things on my mind. I'd told Mike to keep me in view, and I knew he would. The guy tailing him would probably keep him in view, too. That meant I was drawing off both guys – and the longer the better, while Soldier slipped away. I started doing a complete circuit of the fair. It wasn't easy through the crowds, but it wouldn't be easy for the people following me, either.

While I was doing it, I started worrying again. The chap following me had no reason to suspect Soldier – except he'd seen him in the same carriage with me. How about if the fellow had had someone else with him? Mike said there was another guy. How about if they'd all joined up – one following me, one following Mike . . . and one now following Soldier?

It was ridiculous, but the whole thing was ridiculous. I could hardly believe it was happening. It was like the time the gang had come swarming at us with stocking masks. But once I started worrying, I couldn't stop. I knew which way Soldier would go. He'd nip right away to the office block of the old parcels depot. All the buses stopped outside there. They put on special buses from all over town for the fair. He'd get home the quickest way he could, and that was the quickest way.

I started off towards there, doubling back to follow the route he would have to take. It was the opposite end of the fair to the one I'd come in by. All the refreshment stalls were there, and they kept their supplies in vans at the back; it was the outskirts of the parking area.

As I got near it, I began to get nervous in a different way. I knew I'd have to go and look round the back, just to be certain in my own mind. And it was dark there; all the lights and the row were towards the front. It would be easy enough to get caught there and have the stuffing knocked out of you.

And I was dead tired. The guy following me would be tired, too; but he'd looked pretty tough. And he had a couple of grudges to settle with me. I just hoped Mike was not too far behind. I thought I better give Mike a minute or two to get nearer, so I veered away from the vans and kept to the main stream and slowed to a walk to get my breath back.

The snag was, not many people were leaving the fair yet. Crowds were still pouring in off the buses, and anyone going against the tide was easily noticeable. Soldier would have been noticeable. And who would worry if they saw a man dragging a boy away and giving him a clout to keep him quiet? It would look like someone having a row with his father.

I thought I better not leave it any longer. I better look behind the vans after all.

There were pools of deep darkness there. There were piles of crates and boxes around. The back of one of the vans was open, and in the light coming out of it I saw an old chap putting raw potatoes through a chip-slicer. I said, 'Excuse me, have you seen a boy round here?' It was such a wet question he didn't even bother to answer. He just shook his head and shuffled inside with a basket of chips.

Soldier wasn't there, anyway. I couldn't see anybody there, and was turning away with relief when I saw a movement in the car-park beyond; a very quick darting movement like a cat; and then a slower, heavier one, after it. And I got in a pool of shadow and kept very still and watched.

There was lighting strung out over the car-park, weak lighting, just so people could see their way between the cars.

I saw a bloke walking slowly round a station wagon, and he stopped and looked underneath it, and then ran round the other side, and a kid came scuttling out from under, and made another quick dart and got himself behind a car, and I thought, *Oh Gawd*, and my stomach turned over. It was Soldier. He'd got himself trapped in there. I'd have to do something about it.

I moved out of the darkness, and the moment I did, I knew I wasn't alone. The bloke didn't even try to make me think I was. He walked towards me across the narrow shaft of light coming out of the chip van, and I saw that he was still limping. He must have got hurt when he copped the anchor. I jumped back behind a pile of crates, and he came on, rubbing his hands slightly. He was a big heavy chap.

He called, 'Throw over what you've got, and I'll let you go.'

I licked my lips and said, 'I haven't got anything.'

'You little fool, I'll break your neck. I'm warning you – just throw it.'

I threw a crate. I'd seen they were empty, the pile between me and him. He ducked a bit sideways and missed it, and came on fast, and I threw another and caught him on the forehead, and took off. I took off across the car-park, the far side from Soldier. I knew I had to steer him away from Soldier. Soldier would have to look out for himself a bit longer. And so would I.

I knew the geezer was a fast runner, but he was winded now, and limping, and I was pretty sure I could keep him off. I just hoped Soldier could keep his geezer off. He was no runner, Soldier. He'd obviously worked out he had to keep foxing the guy. That's why he was in the car-park, with plenty of cars to hide behind. But you can't do that too often. In the end, the one who is faster will win.

I must have belted on for three or four minutes, and I started panicking then. Three or four minutes in the car-

116

park, three or four minutes before I even went in it . . .
Ample time for Mike to show up. Where the blazes was he?
I'd told him to keep his distance. Couldn't he see we were in
danger here, though? Or had the clot gone and lost me?

I saw I better get nearer Soldier and try and get the film
back while I still had strength to run. The guy was certainly
going to pin him down before long.

I started weaving between the cars towards him, and I
gave him a yell, 'Soldier!' so he would know I was coming
for him and that he didn't have to stay away from me.

He got the point. I saw his little white face glance towards
me, and it was terrified. He was panting hard, almost sobbing.
He skittered round the back of an old Ford, and the guy was
after him, and when I saw him next, he was at the other
side of a little open two-seater sports car, and he was still
looking towards me, and I saw something glinting in his
hand. It was the silver-paper-wrapped film and he was
evidently going to throw it. Only he'd wasted a second or
two, and he'd picked the wrong car. The guy just jumped
over it. He put one hand on a seat-back and simply vaulted
over, and Soldier panicked and dropped the film and it rolled
under the car.

I don't think the guy saw it. I'm quite certain the one following me didn't see it. He was too far behind. I saw it, and
Soldier saw it, and the little dope bent for it, and the guy
was on top of him, and Soldier let out a howl.

I think it was just the breath being knocked out of him.
But the same moment, anyway, there was another howl, and
Mike showed up at last, the big idiot. Because of his leg, he
looks like he's skating when he runs. He came skating up
like someone trying to win the Olympics, and what he did
then, he seemed to do all in one movement, without stop-
ping. He just picked the guy off Soldier. He grabbed him by
his hair and the seat of his pants and sort of threw him

away. Then he bent down and picked Soldier up, and he said seriously, 'Soldier, are you all right, Soldier?'

Soldier had been a bit like a pancake down there, and he didn't have any breath to answer, but he seemed all right, so I didn't bother with him any more. I just got down on my knees and looked under the car. The film had rolled to the far side and I couldn't reach it, and just the same moment the plug-ugly following me steamed up.

He wasn't too quick on the uptake, this geezer. He didn't seem to take in the situation. I suppose for the last few minutes the best thing he could think of in all the world was just to give me a good belting, and he started in on it right away. He caught me by the collar and landed a clout on my head. I think his main idea was to turn me round so he could hit me somewhere else, because I was still on my knees, but he never got the chance.

I didn't see what happened, but the next thing, he was sitting on the ground looking up at Mike, a bit surprised. I already said, Mike is fantastically strong, only he doesn't look it. He just looks tall and skinny. Another thing, he hates fighting. He thinks it's wrong, hitting people. He won't even defend himself – he just covers up like in the lane when the mob got him.

Anyway, the geezer was looking up at him, and he started to his feet again, and Mike said irritably, 'Oh, look, why don't you just go away? I don't want to fight with you.'

The man said 'Why, you young –' I won't put what else he said. He didn't say too much else, anyway. He just leapt at Mike, and Mike pushed him away, and then seemed to go out of his mind. He hadn't noticed it before, but the other guy had grabbed Soldier again. Soldier wasn't saying too much, because he couldn't, and the guy wasn't hitting him or anything. He'd just grabbed him by the throat and had put a hand over his mouth and he was quietly dragging him away. And Mike noticed then.

He gave a sort of snarl and a hop and he brought his arm round and knocked the fellow sideways. He went over like a tree, and Mike picked him off the ground and put him in the sports car.

'Don't you touch that little kid again!' he was roaring at him. 'Don't you dare!' I don't think the fellow could hear him too well. Mike had put him in the sports car upside down, and was talking to his legs. They were kicking in the air a bit.

Then everything went crazy. I don't even know what happened exactly; except that the other guy, the one with a face like a boxer, showed up, so all three of them were there, and Mike seemed to take it into his head they were all there to torment Soldier, and he went berserk. I'd never even seen him so angry, never mind what he did. What he did, he seemed to turn himself into a windmill. Wherever you looked he was swinging and snarling.

The first guy who copped it was the one who knew least about it. It was the old boxer who just came padding up looking for Mike, and he found him right away. Mike bent down and came up again with a most tremendous uppercut, and the bloke practically did a somersault.

He picked himself up a bit dazed, and came forward again, only Mike was busy then with the guy in the sports car, who'd got himself right way up and had jumped at him. Mike hit him while he was still in the air, and if he'd been a cricket ball, Mike would have got a six out of him. Then he gave a bit more attention to the boxer.

I wasn't just standing around while this was going on. The bloke who'd been after me still had this ambition to give me a good clobbering; only he was a bit careful of Mike now, so he tried to get me out of the way first. He hooked an arm round my neck, almost choking me, and started dragging me round the other side of the car.

I wasn't any match for him, but I still had a pair of feet, so I stamped on one of his, hard; and when he hopped a bit, I drew the other foot back and gave him a solid kick in the ankle, and I think it must have been the one he'd copped the anchor with, because I never heard anyone swear harder than he did.

He only did it for a little bit, though, and then stopped sharply, and moved swiftly to the left, because Mike had knocked him there; and then just as swiftly to the right, because Mike had knocked him there, too. And then a car's headlights were on us, and whistles were blowing, and policemen running, and so were these geezers. And Mike said to me, 'Have you got Soldier?' And I said, 'No,' and looked around and he wasn't there. So I looked under the car, and saw the film wasn't there, either, and I said, 'It's O.K., Mike, He's gone. I have to phone him. Let's beat it.'

We skipped round the back of the refreshment vans, and rejoined the crowd; and about five minutes later were on the bus home.

He told me what had happened, when we were moving. He'd come out of Mrs Cripps's, and run across the road and started signalling to me when he suddenly realized four geezers were watching him from the porch of the Temperance Hotel next door. They were under cover, so we hadn't seen them from the window. He didn't recognize them, but he didn't like the look of them, either. So he changed his signal, to tell me not to come down yet, and then he beat it, his idea being to draw them off, so I'd have time to work it out and leave by the back way when I could.

But only two of them followed him, and he didn't know what to do. He was certain I'd put the film back; and he had an idea he might be able to go back and get it himself when Mrs Cripps came back later. So he just kept running. He didn't want to run home and let them know where he lived. So he ran to the fair and tried not to bump into anyone he knew; and I knew all the rest.

13

I rang Soldier as soon as we got in. My mum was at Aunt Freda's, I knew that, so I wouldn't have to lower my voice. I didn't have to lower it, anyway, as it happened. There was no answer, Soldier's end.

That was funny and we worked out various reasons for it. We worked out he might have gone home a long way round to shake off anyone following, or he'd lost his key and couldn't get in, or his phone was out of order. We could check the last, anyway, and I got the operator and did, and there was nothing wrong with the phone.

H'm.

We gave it another ten minutes and tried again, and there was still nothing doing, so we thought we better go round there. We went out the front door at the trot, and there was Soldier coming in the gate.

I said, 'Where the blazes have you been? I been *phoning* you.'

He said, 'I'm sorry, Woolcott. I thought I better come instead. I couldn't go home.'

'Why not?'

'He got my cap, that man.'

'What about it?'

'My name and address is in it.'

'Oh.' He does these things. He has his name and address in his gym shoes, even. 'Well, come in, then.'

We all went in and I said, 'You got the film?'

'No.'

'What do you mean, no?' I was so nervy I nearly jumped on him. 'I looked under the car. It wasn't there.'

'I got it, I got it,' he said. He was trying to calm me down so hard, he was stroking my arm. 'I just haven't got it now.'

'Where is it?'

'Nixon's got it.'

'What!'

'Well, I thought – I mean,' he said, a bit crestfallen. I think he thought he just had to say that and I'd jump for joy. 'I had to think fast, and they were chasing me, and nobody was chasing him, and it seemed a good idea.'

It was a lousy idea. I knew it. I remembered what I'd said to Nixon. He'd do something wild, to show off. He'd take over the whole plan himself.

'I didn't want him to know anything about it,' I said.

'Well, that's all right. He doesn't.'

'No, but he'll make out that he does. He's a big mouth. It's not safe with him.'

'I'm telling you,' Soldier said. 'He doesn't know *anything* about it. He doesn't even know he's got it – though he might by now.'

'What you talking about?'

'He won a bag of chocolates. They're wrapped in silver paper,' Soldier said. 'So is the film.'

He'd shoved the film in the bag! He'd asked Nixon to show what he'd won, and slipped it in and given him it back. 'He said he was going home soon. So the film will be going there, too.'

'But he might lose the bag!'

'Oh, no, he won't,' Soldier said confidently. 'Not Nixon. And he said he won't eat the stuff till tomorrow, so that's fine.'

'Because he didn't want to give you any. He could be eating it now!'

'He won't eat a film,' Soldier said.

'But he'll open it.'

'Let him. He'll see what it is, and it'll be safe.'

'Oh, Gawd !' I said. 'Soldier – it's undeveloped, that film. If he opens it, he'll ruin it.'

Soldier's face went grey and he said, 'Oh, no. You never told me . . .'

I was already at the phone. I tried to think what to tell him, as I dialled. It was hard to say anything to him, after what I'd said. I remembered he called me Jim when he had something serious to say, so I thought I'd do it with him. Then I wondered what to say if his old man answered instead. But it wasn't his old man, it was him, and he said, 'Dr Nixon's home.'

I said urgently, 'Ron. It's Jim.'

'Goodbye, then,' he said.

I said, 'Please, Ron. Listen –'

He hung up.

'Oh, no,' Soldier said. He'd heard the click. He'd kept on saying it, anyway.

'We better go round there,' Mike said.

'It's too urgent. There's no time. He could be –'

'I'll ring,' Soldier said.

He did. The phone rang several times without being answered, then Mrs Nixon answered, and Soldier asked if Ron was there. Apparently he was, but he wouldn't come to the phone till he knew who wanted him, and when he did he sounded bad-tempered. We heard him.

'Yeah, what is it?' he said.

'Nixon – have you opened the chocolates yet?' Soldier said.

'Why?'

He hadn't. I knew that tone. I knew him pretty well.

Soldier told him why. He told him slowly and quietly,

and there was a bit of a pause when he finished, then Nixon said, 'Hang on,' and went away.

His voice was different when he came back, and I knew that tone, too. It was cocky. He said, 'O.K. then, Soldier.'

'You've got it?'

'Sure.'

'Don't open it! It's undeveloped.'

'Don't worry about a thing, kid,' Nixon said.

I bit my lip and said, 'See if he'll talk to me. I have to talk to him. He'll do something crazy.'

'Nixon,' Soldier said. 'Woolcott's here. He *has* to have a few words with you. Please don't say no.'

'O.K., I won't,' Nixon said. 'Just give him a few from me. Say if it's about any of my prizes, I'll take his earlier advice. I'll just keep 'em to myself.' He was sniggering as he hung up.

Soldier went and made a pot of tea, and Mike walked up and down and I went quietly out of my mind.

'It'll be all right,' Mike kept saying. 'It'll be all right, you'll see.'

'It won't. He'll try and do it himself, the fool!' I was scaring myself with all the things that could go wrong if he developed it himself. He messed about with photography. I'd seen some of his efforts. And Moggy had said the exposure was 'delicate'.

'How about ringing Moggy, then?' Mike said.

'What can I say?'

'Tell him we got it.'

'He'll want to know where.'

'No, he won't,' Soldier said, coming in with the tea just then. 'Not on the phone, he won't. He'll want to see you. And you'll have to put him off. It's not safe to go there.

They could have that place covered by now. You'll have to tell him all that without actually saying it.'

'How?'

'He'll give you a lead. He'll have things to tell you, anyway, if he knows you're not coming, and he'll be careful how he does that. Haven't you got to call yourself Bob or something?'

'Yeah,' I'd forgotten that. 'H'm,' I said, and phoned Moggy. They asked who wanted him, and I said Bob, and a moment later Moggy was there.

'Hello, Bob. How's everything, Bob?' Moggy said.

'Everything's fine, Mr Morgan.'

'All happy and healthy and present and correct?'

'Everything.'

'Well, that's nice. That's very nice,' Moggy said. 'You must drop by and see me.'

I coughed. 'Well, I'd like to. But I expect you'll have visitors around. You know.'

'Oh. H'm. Yes. I see,' Moggy said. 'Dammit,' he said as an afterthought.

'Yes.'

'I'd like to get out of this place. Boring here. Not even any pictures to look at,' he said.

'No.'

'Modern pictures. You know, when I planned my picture show, my idea was to get there early, to catch people's interest before they passed on to other things. That's always an excellent idea, Bob.'

'I see.'

'Of course, a lot of modern art work, you know, it's not really – not really ready to show yet.'

'You mean, it's not developed, Mr Morgan.'

'That's exactly what I mean. Exactly. I'm glad you got the point, Bob. And it's got to be, you see. I certainly wouldn't put anything before the public that wasn't developed. *Properly* developed, you see. Dammit,' he said.

'Yes. I suppose some people develop a bit – a bit slow, eh?' I said desperately. 'Or fast, or something. I don't know too much about it, you see. But I know people that do.'

'Yes. Yes. Quite. I'm just trying to think,' Moggy said. 'As far as I remember,' he said slowly, 'I know someone who developed when he was sixty-eight.'

'Sixty-eight?' I said. I was holding the phone away from my ear. I saw Soldier was writing it down.

'Sixty-eight. I'm pretty sure of it. It took about ten minutes for an image to form in his mind before he had an idea of his picture.'

'Ten minutes, eh?'

'Ten minutes. Of course, he had a high ID 2.'

'A high what?'

'That was a joke,' Moggy said. 'I meant IQ.'

'What was the joke?'

'I said ID 2. I mean IQ – you know, the intelligence test thing. It just shows how your mind wanders, lying in bed. It's funny, isn't it?'

Soldier had written down ID 2 and was looking at it. Then he looked at me. 'Check it,' he whispered.

'I didn't get the joke,' I said to Moggy.

'Well, I meant IQ, but I *said* ID 2. That's what I *said*,' Moggy said.

'I see. Ha-ha. ID 2.'

'Exactly,' Moggy said. 'Ha-ha-ha. And another thing with this character, it took him fifteen minutes to fix the thing in his mind after he'd developed the idea.'

'Fifteen minutes, eh?'

'Fifteen minutes. But the most important thing,' he said suddenly, 'the absolutely vital thing was that he believed in keeping all his ideas together. He wanted them all to show just as they occurred to him. I just hope that makes sense to you, Bob.'

'I think it does, Mr Morgan.'

'I sincerely hope so, Bob. It's very important.'

'He didn't believe in chopping them up.'

'That's exactly it,' Moggy said with relief.

'O.K., then, Mr Morgan.'

'Yes. I wish I could get out of here. All the best, then, Bob, if you're doing anything tomorrow, I expect you'll do it *early*.'

'Yeah, all right,' I said. I was beginning to get a bit fed up with all this. 'Goodbye, Mr Morgan . . . Did you get all that?' I said to Soldier as I put the phone down.

He'd got it. He'd got some weird little bits of information on the paper. Once we sorted it out, it was simple enough, though. The film had to be developed for ten minutes at sixty-eight degrees in some stuff called ID 2. Then it had to be fixed for fifteen minutes. Moggy didn't want it cut up in any way, but just kept in one roll. And he wanted it at the Inquiry early, before they passed on to other business.

'O.K.,' Soldier said, and picked up the phone and dialled Nixon again.

But Nixon wouldn't come to the phone this time. He was up in his room with the door locked, and he'd told his mother he couldn't be interrupted for about half an hour. She thought he must be doing some photography.

Mike took charge round about then. He ran out and whistled up a taxi, and we all belted down to Nixon's in it.

I'd been up to his room before, so his mother let us up. He still wouldn't open the door, though, and he wouldn't talk to me at all. He talked to Mike and Soldier from the other side of the door.

He hadn't started developing yet. He was still getting the

film in the developing tank. I'd seen him doing it before up there. He hasn't got a proper darkroom. He hasn't got a daylight loader, either. He just covers the windows and the cracks in the door with blankets, and then gets in bed and does the whole thing under the covers. It's a fiddly business getting a film in the tank in pitch darkness. With all the preparations, it usually took him half an hour, and that's where he was at now.

'Well, listen,' Mike said. 'We been speaking to Moggy. There's special instructions for that film. Have you got a pencil?'

'I can't put the light on yet.'

'O.K., we'll wait.'

'No, you won't,' Nixon said, suspiciously. 'I'll tell you what. Hang on a minute, and you can slip it under the door.'

'It isn't really written out properly,' Soldier said.

'Well, write it out properly,' Nixon said. 'You'll have time.'

I cursed a bit while Soldier carefully copied the right bits out. He did it on the banister. Nixon certainly wouldn't be opening the door any time we were there. He'd taken over the whole scheme himself, as I thought. Mr Big.

We heard him shuffling about in there, and he said 'O.K. Shove it under.'

Soldier shoved it under. 'Does ID 2 mean anything to you?' he said.

'Yeah,' Nixon said. 'It's a fine-grain film developer.'

'Have you got any?'

Nixon didn't say anything for a bit. He was reading through the rest of it.

'No, I haven't,' he said. He sounded worried.

'Well, you've got to have it. Don't do it without. You can ruin it.'

'H'm.'

'Is it possible to get some?' Mike said.

'Well. It's Easter Monday. Shops are shut.'

'Doesn't you old man know any chemists?'

'I was thinking of that . . .'

Mike said, 'Look – if you want to make a phone call or anything, we could pick the stuff up for you.'

'No. No, it's O.K.,' Nixon said. I knew he'd say that. He had to do it all. That way he'd get all the praise. And there were fifty different ways he could wreck it.

I said desperately, 'Ron, it's too important for –'

'Oh, shove off, everybody. I got things to do.'

'We can argue some other time. But now –'

'And you shove off in particular,' he said.

'But I've got to tell Moggy something.'

'Tell him what you want.'

'How will we know if you've done it?'

'You won't, will you?'

I nearly smashed the door in, but Mike grabbed me and said, 'Nixon, listen. Promise you'll ring when you've done it. Promise that.'

'O.K. Only someone else better take the call. Not *him*.'

I said it before, but it's never going to be any different with him : he keeps a quarrel going a long time, Nixon.

We hung about at my place waiting for him to call, and working out what could go wrong. Plenty could go wrong, and plenty still had to be done. The film had to be got into the Inquiry for one thing. It was opening at eleven in the morning, in the Council Chamber of the Town Hall.

I looked around for the newspaper to see the arrangements, and we read it together. It was a big story in the newspaper : whatever was decided was going to change the town completely. There were millions and millions of pounds involved, and thousands of people interested.

There was a very limited amount of room for the public in the Council Chamber; so they'd rigged up closed-circuit television in the hall below; it was the hall off the one where Moggy's exhibition was being held.

There'd be crowds inside, crowds outside . . . probably including a few characters we knew already. How to get the film past them? And inside? And produce it before the committee?

And where was the film, anyway? It was nine o'clock and Nixon still hadn't rung. There were a couple of calls for my mother; and then one from her. She wanted to see if I'd eaten yet.

'I'll have something later,' I said.

'There's the salmon in the fridge.'

'Yeah. O.K.'

'And that nice salad. You can have that.'

'Fine.'

'Unless – is Mike with you?'

'Yeah.'

'Well, leave the salmon. There's not enough for two. You can have the hamburgers. And baked beans, if you want. Do you want that?'

'Yeah. All right.'

'Not yeah. Yes.'

'Yes. It will be beautiful,' I said. We'd already eaten the hamburgers.

'There isn't anybody else there, is there?'

'Soldier's here.'

'Oh. Well, in that case I think you'd all better have soup and sandwiches. There's plenty of things in the fridge. Or eggs, if you want. Would you sooner have eggs?'

'I think so. Yes. Definitely,' I said. I thought I'd blow my mind if she kept working her way through the fridge.

'All right, then. Don't make a mess. And you can have ice-cream after. You'll find it in the top.'

'Ice-cream. Lovely. Wonderful. Oh, thank you, Mum,' I said. 'Good night,' and hung up fast.

'Ice-cream?' Soldier said. He's a hungry little devil. He'd been seriously reading the paper but he always seemed to keep a bit of his mind open for food.

'Yeah, you want some?'

'I dont' mind.'

We all had some.

There wasn't much else to do. Mr Big still hadn't phoned.

He didn't phone till ten, and he phoned then to let us know he was going to bed.

'What?' Soldier said. 'But listen – is everything O.K.?'

'Mm? Oh. Yeah,' Nixon said casually.

'But what about tomorrow?'

'What about tomorrow?'

'I mean – we've got to get it *in* there.'

'*We* haven't. I have. Don't worry your little head about it.'

'But listen – Nixon –'

'And another thing. Don't bother ringing up any more because I won't answer. And don't come round, because I won't open the door. Pleasant dreams,' Nixon said, and hung up.

What we decided was this: since he'd taken control, he had to be given his chance – and since nobody seemed to be on to him, it might be the best chance, anyway. *Somebody* had to get the thing into the hall. We couldn't all carry it between us. But we'd all be there, anyway. We'd go early, and if it turned out that someone *was* on to him, at least we'd be around to help.

Soldier didn't want to go home, because of his cap, so he

slept at my place. And Mike didn't fancy walking home in the dark, either, so he phoned for a taxi to come and get him. He'd paid for the other taxi, too.

'What's this – you the last of the big spenders?' I said.

'What is there to lose?' Mike said.

He'd turned a bit gloomy again the last hour or two. So had I. And Soldier wasn't exactly laughing boy. We all knew Nixon was handling something he didn't understand, really, and after all we'd been through it was no fun waiting for him to wreck it.

We got to the Town Hall at nine, and found a queue of about fifty people there already, and a dozen policemen looking after them. We didn't see anyone following us, but not half a minute after we joined the queue, a couple of the guys were there behind us. One was the guy who'd followed me yesterday, and he had a black eye now. We didn't know the other.

They didn't make any sign they recognized us (four or five people were in between), but after a while, Black Eye's partner wandered towards the head of the queue and had a word with a couple of other guys there, and they turned and looked at us. We didn't recognize them, either. But they all knew us now; two in front and two behind.

That was O.K. It was what we wanted. We were taking the heat off Nixon. What I'd wanted to tell Nixon was not to give any hint he knew us. He had to keep well away; but he had to make sure he'd get in the hall, too. This was a question of timing and careful planning, because the hall would only hold so many. He had to leave it till a late moment, so there'd be plenty of people in the queue, including plenty of kids – quite a few were coming from school because the Cobbler and the Board of Governors were on the committee. But he mustn't leave it too late to get in.

133

There was also the question of what he'd do with the film once he got in. By leaving it till late, it meant he wouldn't get in the Council Chamber, anyway. There were only a few dozen places for the public there. What was he going to do with it in the hall below? Jump up and yell? Stand on his head? Run to a policeman? We hadn't discussed any of it. He'd have worked out something flashy, though; I knew him; something that would show what a genius he was – and put the whole scheme in danger.

But an even bigger worry was that he might not leave it till late; that he might come swanking up with the thing and show he knew us, and get himself clobbered before he even got near the hall.

By ten o'clock that danger seemed to be over, anyway. Hundreds had turned up by then, and photographers were busy taking pictures. There was no sign of Nixon.

By half past, we wouldn't even have known if he was there or not. A big scrambling mass of people had gathered, apart from the queue, just to watch. Various important geezers, including politicians and the mayor and the Cobbler and other Committee members arrived, and people kept an aisle open for them. They walked up it, giving a big hello to the photographers, and getting cheered or booed by different sections of the crowd.

At quarter to eleven, they let the first few in the queue through to the Council Chamber. When all the places were filled there, they let the rest through to the hall below. That was us.

'What we going to do?' Mike said.

'We better go in – what else?'

'You don't reckon I ought to have a look up the queue, see if he's there?'

'Of course not. Stay away from him.'

'And if he isn't there?' Soldier said.

'He better be,' I said.

The two guys near the head of the queue were politely giving up their places to others till they saw what we were going to do. They went in just ahead of us as we moved.

We filed through Moggy's exhibition and went in the hall and saw it was all set out with hundreds of chairs. They had a big screen rigged like in a cinema, and the cameras were already on. You could see the geezers on the committee sitting chatting at a big U-shaped table.

There were several ushers in the hall, and they showed us where to go, and we shuffled along a row, and the guys covering us shuffled along it, too. They were pretty twitchy now, and they didn't pretend that they weren't watching us. They hardly took their eyes off us. I wondered what they'd do if we did suddenly produce it. Jump on us, start a lot of confusion, burn it? They wouldn't have the chance, anyway. I saw the guy who'd followed me was still limping a bit, and the look he gave me from his black eye wasn't very nice.

The hall filled up fast, and it was impossible in the shifting mass of people to see if Nixon was there or not. He certainly wasn't within any visible row of us.

Then the thing started and we waited on tenterhooks, and an old geezer called Sir Frederick Twite got up on the screen (he was the chairman the Government had appointed) and said he wasn't going to make a speech, and made one for about four hours, except it was twenty minutes exactly on my watch. He said they were all deeply conscious of the momentous decisions that had to be taken, and while he was saying it, Dr Nixon hurried in with his bag and apologized, and Sir Twite made a crack about how sick patients came before sick towns, and Mike and Soldier and I looked at each other the same moment and just grinned.

So that's what he'd done. He'd given it to his dad. He'd

had it taken right to the Council Chamber by his own personal messenger. I don't know why we hadn't thought of it. We'd thought of everything else, we hadn't thought of that. It was neat, and it was cool, and I had to hand it to him, and we just sat there grinning at each other, and the geezers on each side of us looked at us and at each other and started shuffling their feet.

Dr Nixon put his glasses on, and we waited for him to say, 'O.K., hold it, Twite. I got a little something here to show you,' but he just took his handkerchief out and blew his nose and started nodding seriously at what Twite was saying.

Then Twite sat down, and Dr Nixon ought to have stood up, but he didn't. The Town Clerk stood up, and he said before they went into serious discussions he'd like to say a word about a matter that had been a good deal in the newspapers.

He said they'd all heard about a mysterious document that had been found, and that had just as mysteriously disappeared. A great many sensational theories had been aired about this document, which was no doubt a very beautiful old document. What he would like to say was that it had not been brought before the committee, and no copy of it had been brought, and that it was therefore his duty to inform the press and the public that they need not expect any further *fantastic revelations* (he chuckled a bit, and several geezers chuckled with him) and that what they would be discussing was hard facts.

Then he nodded at the chairman and sat down, and Twite said he was happy to call on Mr Wilfred Carter of the Carter Development Corporation, and a character got up and started talking about skyscrapers.

The three of us looked at each other in a sick sort of way. The idiot hadn't given it to his old man. He'd tried to be clever some other way, and had messed it up. He was probably hanging about outside the hall now, unable to get in.

Mike whispered to me, 'I'm going out.'

'No, you're not!'

They'd follow him if he went out. The film was still a film. If it wasn't produced today, it could be produced some other day. Except Moggy had said to get in early with it, before they passed on to other business. Maybe they could rule it out of order or something, if it was left too long. Who knew what they could do?

The geezer was still droning on about skyscrapers when an usher came in the picture and whispered in Dr Nixon's ear. He got up and went out of the picture.

We looked at each other again. The geezers on each side were looking at each other, too. Their eyes were going there and back from the screen, to us, to each other. They obviously didn't know what to make of it.

They didn't have too long to find out. Dr Nixon came back in the picture quite soon. He came back fast, and he picked up his bag and started throwing everything out of it.

The skyscraper expert was in the middle of the picture, and you could only see Dr Nixon in the background. You could see him quite well, though. He was tugging at something at the bottom of his bag. It seemed to be taped there. Then he pulled it out, and looked at it, and said 'Excuse me.'

Mr Carter of the Carter Development Corporation stopped in the middle of a word and looked round, a bit irritated, and then carried on about skyscrapers.

'I'm sorry,' Dr Nixon said. 'I'm afraid I must interrupt the proceedings. I'm really sorry.'

He didn't look too sorry. He looked as if he was going to die laughing.

So Nixon had done it that way: with a single phone call. Even his old man hadn't known. Nobody else had known; only him.

As I'd thought. Flashy.

There isn't too much more to put. I mean, there's plenty, but it's been a big pain in the neck putting all this already.

They didn't knock down Auldhouses. They didn't put any skyscrapers up on the market area, either. Our playing fields are going there. The swine who always drives off to Rennisham too early won't have to bother much longer. He can just stay there all day if he wants. And Moggy's doing very well. He isn't with us any more. With all the publicity, he didn't have to hang around waiting for Lepic to give him an exhibition in his rat-hole. He got one about a month later in London. He sold every picture in the exhibition. He even managed to track down the anchor, and asked Mike's opinion again, and Mike said he thought an anchor was a very useful thing, so he stuck it back on his picture, and sold that, too, which shows you what kind of twits they must have in London. And art there seemed such a reasonable business, he gave up his job at the school.

Of course, Mike was sick at him going, but they're in touch with each other. I forgot to say, he's still at Turner's, Mike. The first thing Moggy did when they let him out of hospital, he ran round to the Cobbler and practically made him eat Mike's report. He pointed out what I said already, that if it came to people making contributions to the school, the only visible one anyone had made for about four hundred years had been made by Mike in figuring out where Mary Turner's fields had been.

He's still in our class. I wouldn't say he's the biggest genius going, and if there's a head waiter who needs a wash anywhere in French, Mike is still the one who's going to find him. But he gets by. I mean, who's a genius?

And Soldier keeps on being Soldier. And Nixon . . . is Nixon. He can't help doing what he does, and despite everything he's still my friend. He didn't show up too good in what I had to put here, but there's more to him than that, and maybe I'll tell it some time. But what I had to tell here is what happened, and that's about it.

also by David Line

RUN FOR YOUR LIFE

'I want to report a murder,' Soldier said.

'Where?'

'I don't know where,' Soldier said.

'Who's been murdered?'

'Nobody yet,' Soldier said. 'That's what I want to tell you.'

Nobody said anything while he got it out. The other policemen stopped what they were doing and listened, but none believed Soldier had really overheard the men planning a murder.

But the men did commit the murder, and they knew only one way to stop the boys telling what they had seen. . . .

This was David Line's first suspense story for children, and it was serialised on television as *Soldier and Me*.

WHAT ABOUT ME?

Gertie Evenhuis

Four years of war – blackout, gunfire, threadbare clothes and harsh German voices blaring through the streets, voices that sounded frightening even when they sang – in that time Dirk had grown into a serious eleven-year-old who desperately wanted to have a share in the secret goings-on of his elder brother, to *do* something to push the German invaders out of their lovely Amsterdam.

But when he saw the deadly result of his actions he knew that the fear of the Germans he had felt before was just a shadow of the terror he was feeling now – for his brother, for himself, and above all for the teacher whose life he had put in such peril.

THE PERILOUS DESCENT

Bruce Carter

The descent was perilous all right – by parachute, and under strange conditions. Johnny Wild and Danny Black were two airmen returning from a bombing raid at the end of the war. They were shot down over the North Sea, but managed to reach a sandbank. They crawled ashore to rest, fell asleep in a little hollow, and woke to find that the dip seemed deeper. They tried to scramble out, but found the sand slipping beneath them, going down, and they with it, down and down.

What happened after that has the powerful thrill of a Wells romance or a Jules Verne yarn – yet it is very much a story of today. The tension never slackens, the suspense holds to the very end.

AN AMERICAN GHOST

Chester Aaron

Finding yourself alone in half a house, floating down river towards the Mississippi, with no-one to come after you because it seems certain you are drowned, is daunting enough for 13-year-old Albie, but he has two other terrors to contend with. First there is the American Ghost (or deadly mountain lion), which is also in the floating prison, raging with hunger and seeing Albie as the only food for herself and her cubs, and then a bunch of looters are determined to kidnap him for a ransom.

During the seven weeks that Albie faces one difficulty after another, he finds in himself a courage and resourcefulness neither he nor his family would ever have guessed at. This is a really memorable book, both a first-rate adventure and an exceptional animal story.

If you have enjoyed reading this book and would like to know about others which we publish, why not join the Puffin Club? You will be sent the club magazine, *Puffin Post*, four times a year and a smart badge and membership book. You will also be able to enter all the competitions. For details of cost and an application form, send a stamped addressed envelope to:

The Puffin Club Dept A
Penguin Books Limited
Bath Road
Harmondsworth, Middlesex